Titania's Suitor

Titania's Suitor

C. L. Shore

Digital ISBN: 978-0-9862223-1-3

Print ISBN: 978-0-9862223-0-6

Printed by CreateSpace

Acknowledgments

This story has been "under construction" for an extended period, and I'd like to thank those friends and family members who facilitated its becoming reality. Most of all, I'd like to thank my friend Linda; without her inspiration, *Titania's Suitor* would not be much of a story. My friends Janice and Janet read early versions and gave me the confidence to continue writing. My family members, husband John, daughter Eve, son Ben and daughter-in-law Aoi, helped read early drafts and gave suggestions for improvement. My grandson provided valuable assistance with technical aspects including cover design.

This book is dedicated to pioneering women in the sciences, past, present, and future.

Part One
November

To: Hansen, V
Date: Wednesday, November 26
From: Stone, Charlotte P
Subject: It's finally here

Veronica,

Well, the deed is finally done. Pete moved out last night. And even though we both knew it was coming, it was very, very hard. Lauren cried and cried, before and after Pete left. I thought I would cry, too; but I couldn't. I guess I've cried all the tears I've got. It will take a while for them to replenish themselves.

To top it all off, Lauren will go with Pete to his parents' over Thanksgiving weekend. He'll pick her up early tomorrow morning. It makes sense, since I'll have her for every week during the school year and every other weekend. We're determined to keep things amicable, for Lauren's sake and for ours. It's crazy, but we both feel like we still love each other. But this break-up seemed inevitable since I started back to school almost two years ago. We seemed to be arguing constantly once that change took place. Things kept going downhill. But somehow, I don't think dropping out of grad school is right. For one thing, I have the government scholarship. If I quit now, I'd have to pay it back. Besides that, when I took that scholarship, I gave my word that I would try my best to complete this program and learn how to do research. I signed a contract of sorts. And I *want* to finish. Maybe I'll put myself on the fast track and try to finish as quickly as possible.

Anyhow, fortunately (?) I do have an invitation to an "adults only" Thanksgiving with some of the other research assistants. They are almost all younger than me by at least seven years. But we know each other well, and there won't be any kids around to make me miss Lauren. I'll bring a salad, try to enjoy the company and/or watch football. Beats being alone on the holiday. I don't have the money to fly home to Chicago, and I don't want to drive by myself... too much time alone to think.

So here I am working on this set of data, trying to scan it for errors. I'm not in the best frame of mind to do that. I even did this intelligence test that popped up after checking my email. It turned out to be longer than I thought. After investing so much time in it, I wanted to know my score. I had to give my email address in order to get the results. And all it told me is that I did "very well." I thought I at least deserved to know the items I got right!

Oh well, back to work. The office is almost deserted. Today is a holiday for students, but not staff. Still, very few people are here. You know how it is, everyone wants a jump-start on the holiday.

You are so lucky, you'll have both of your kids and their kids around you on Thanksgiving! Be grateful!! By the way, thanks for the book on anger in relationships. It has been helpful already.

Have a good Turkey Day – Charlotte

To: Stone, Charlotte P
Date: Wednesday, November 26
From: Hansen, V
Subject: Re: It's finally here

Charlotte,

I am so proud of you. I'm not taking sides with the breakup – not at all. But I'm proud of you for getting through this event and keeping your head together. I know it is difficult, since I've been through it twice, with the same person. But, I didn't love the guy at the times of the breakups and you do. It has got to be an awful experience.

I'm glad you have somewhere to go for the holiday. I would invite you over, but I will be at Allen's with his kids. Allen is going to try this new turkey stuffing that he found in an Italian cookbook. He is quite the chef. I guess single fatherhood can force that role on you! Helen is playing the martyred ex-wife right now, but I'm sure she'll snap out of it when she has the kids on Christmas. She is such a whiner!

Yes, the anger book really helped me out, too. I also started journaling when Stan and I broke up. I also saw a counselor, who really helped me get my life in perspective. You may want to consider it at some point.

You are being true to yourself in this situation. You will not regret it, even though it's hard for you now. Trust me on this one! I'll be home late Thursday night, and I only have to work a half-day on Friday (in the morning). So call me if you need me.

Veronica

To: Hansen, V
Date: Thursday, November 27
From: Stone, Charlotte P
Subject: Post-holiday blues

Hello Veronica,

I feel so sad right now. My apartment is so quiet. Not only is Lauren gone, no one else seems to be in the building, either. It is almost spooky around here.

I guess I'm glad that I went to the Thanksgiving celebration. It was at Jake's place. He only lives a half a mile from here. He is actually an MD, but works on several research projects, and is basically the same age as a lot of the research assistants. I think he has even dated a couple of them, occasionally. He's a nice guy, very dedicated to his career, but not a Type A personality. He is from Hawaii and didn't even consider going home for the holiday. He had invited a couple of male MD friends. One (a pediatrician named Max) seemed to go out of his way to talk to me a lot. I was polite, but definitely NOT in a mood to flirt. I hope I wasn't too much of a wet blanket. My two fellow doctoral student/research assistant friends were there: Susan and Becky. Both seemed to have a good time. They brought some wine, but they were the only ones who drank any. One of Jake's friends was on call, and I just didn't feel like it. We played a couple of board games and watched football in addition to eating. A lot of the food came pre-prepared from a deli. But it wasn't bad at all. It was a much better alternative than staying home by myself all day.

I need to start analyzing the data for my dissertation, but I am just not in the mood right now. Can't concentrate well. I'll try to start out fresh tomorrow. Lauren won't be back until 8 AM on Sunday.

Interestingly, I haven't heard a word from my in-laws since Pete and I have been having problems. Pete says he has told them a little about the situation, so they wouldn't be blind-sided if we did break up. Since he told me that, they have not spoken to me directly. I hope that changes. After all, their granddaughter is my daughter, and we need to be civil to each other. I know part of it is that my mother-in-law doesn't think that women should have careers in science, or go on for advanced degrees. She probably thinks I deserve what I'm getting, whatever that is!

Hope your Thanksgiving was nice. It sounded like fun. I wouldn't mind trying Allen's cooking some time. And how is Van? Is he treating you well? He'd better!

Take care!

Charlotte

To: Stone, Charlotte P
Date: Friday, November 28
From: Hansen, V
Subject: Turkey Day

Hey there,

Well, all things considered, I think you did very well! You went out, you socialized, you felt better than you would have if you stayed at home. Flirting would have been a bad idea this soon after a breakup. (Besides, you are still married!) Just stay friendly (which you did).

I'm at work now. Nothing is going on here. There are no admissions scheduled, so I'm basically here just in case there is an emergency psychiatric case. I'm tidying up my cubbyhole, and looking up some references to some of the newer psych drugs.

Allen's house was fun. The kids were all over, and it was very chaotic for a while. Then everyone had some turkey, and the kids crawled off to separate corners to nap. Allen and I had the kitchen cleaned up by the time they were ready to play again.

Has Lauren called you at all? By the way, where is Pete living now?

Take care of yourself!! Read a good novel, take a bubble bath, buy a new lipstick!

Veronica

To: Stone, Charlotte P
Date: Friday, November 28
From: Stone, Peter E
Subject: Lauren

Charlotte:

Lauren has a fever. I'm not sure what to do. Should I give her acetaminophen, ibuprofen, or both? I tried to call your cell, but you must have it turned off. No one answered at the apartment either.

Pete

To: Hansen, V
Date: Friday, November 28
From: Stone, Charlotte P
Subject: MEN!!

Veronica,

I can't believe it! I just got off the phone with Pete. Lauren has a fever of 103.5! Pete and his mother couldn't figure out what to do! It is not rocket science to go to the store, buy some children's acetaminophen or ibuprofen, read the directions, and give the medicine. But they hadn't done that. (How ironic that Pete works in pharmaceutical research!) Pete had been trying to call my cell, which I've turned off since I didn't expect any calls from anyone. (My mom can't remember my cell phone number). So, I told him, step by step what to do. If the fever doesn't come down, I told him to take Lauren to urgent care, since the pediatrician's office is closed for the weekend. I offered to come and get her, but no dice. I will call in an hour to see if she's improving. Her only other symptom is a sore throat. He didn't see any white patches on her tonsils, but I'm not sure if he really knows what to look for.

In answer to your question, Pete has moved in with his parents. He says it is temporary. Although our budgets will be tighter living apart, he could afford to rent a small apartment. I'll bet it doesn't happen soon, if at all. I'm sure it is much easier for him to live with his mom and dad. His mother will probably even do his laundry for him! She probably is telling him that if I hadn't gone back to graduate school, he would still be a homeowner. Thanks to my poor sense of priorities, Pete is now homeless. At least that is how Mommie Dearest sees it. But, maybe Pete doesn't want to commit to a lease at this point, because we might get back together, eventually. I gave up trying to figure him out a long time ago!

Your Thanksgiving sounded like a success. But you still didn't mention Van. I need to meet him sometime. He sounds special.

My computer is so slow lately. I'm wondering if I have a virus, but can't afford any computer repair right now. As long as it keeps working...

Charlotte

To: Stone, Charlotte P
Date: Saturday, November 29
From: Hansen, V
Subject: Re: MEN!!

Hi Charlotte,

Hope by now you've heard from Pete or maybe even talked to Lauren, and that things are going better. It is probably difficult when you can't see Lauren yourself. Men are not very good at managing sick kids, at least in my experience. I can remember coming home from work and finding Stan watching Anna play with Legos on the floor. Her face was as red as a beet and her temp was over 105! I rushed her to the doctor. Turned out to be a virus.

I'm just puttering around the house. Trying to get some fall housecleaning done before the weather turns more winter-like.

Van usually calls or e-mails every evening. I didn't hear from him Thurs. but he was at his daughter's. He has a good relationship with both kids. He has many interesting stories to tell about being on the police force, and different things about his childhood. He is a great storyteller. That is one reason why I enjoy being with him, I could listen to his stories for hours. And I love working with him on cases in his private investigator business. He pays me well, too. We are actually going to go out for dinner tonight. He hates movies, though. Believe it or not, the last one he saw was "Patton"!

Hang in there. Lauren will be back tomorrow.

Veronica

To: Hansen, V
Date: Saturday, Nov. 29
From: Stone, Charlotte P
Subject: Update

Hi Veronica,

Well, I did get to talk to Lauren last night. It was about two hours after she took some acetaminophen. She sounded pretty much like her normal self, and that was reassuring to me.

After I hung up, it struck me again how quiet my apartment is without the presence of a seven-year-old. I'm probably the only one in my entire building. Finally, I cried. Probably buckets. Gallons. I should go out and buy a gallon of Gatorade to replace all of the fluids I've lost. For the past couple of days, I've felt so strange and disconnected. I just couldn't cry. I didn't even feel that sad – I just felt kind of mechanical. But last night I felt overwhelmingly sad, mostly because I felt so alone! But, in a weird kind of way, it felt kind of good to cry, because I knew I would have to feel the sadness sooner or later. I was getting on with it.

After my good cry, I did feel like I could focus on something for at least a little while. I got out my data and started looking through it for patterns and errors. Undoubtedly, this data will become the basis for my dissertation. Right now, I'm just looking through a small part of it. If Pete were here, I'd pick his brain as a research pharmacist. (I'm still appalled that he couldn't figure out to give Lauren a dose of acetaminophen.) I suppose I could call one of his coworkers at SomaRx that I've met, and ask him a few general questions. But, I hesitate to do that yet. Anyhow, I think this research could make a contribution; possibly a discovery that could really make a difference in some people's lives. But what do I know? I'm just a graduate nursing student trying to finish a PhD! I suppose many graduate students get grandiose ideas about their dissertations.

Well, I'm tired out now. I think I'll watch some TV that doesn't require any emotional or intellectual effort. Between the cry and the data analysis, I'm pretty brain dead.

Thanks for all of your support.

Charlotte

To: Stone, Charlotte P
Date: Saturday, November 29
From: Stone, Peter E
Subject: Lauren

Charlotte – I'll have Lauren in front of the building at 0800 SHARP. Please be downstairs on time.

Pete

To: Stone, Charlotte P
Date: Saturday, November 29
From: Hansen, V
Subject: A little cheer

Hi Charlotte,

I knew the time for your good cry would come. I even cried when I
left Stan and I had been planning for it and even looking forward to
it FOR MONTHS! I'd been sleeping on the couch all summer, but I
decided to wait to move out until the kids went back to school, so
they would have a routine in their daily lives after the breakup. So I
left just after Labor Day. I had my own apartment for over eight
months, unbeknownst to Stan. My Dad had given me some money
and I asked him to loan me a little more. Stan was going to undercut
my ability to finish nursing school, and I couldn't allow that to
happen. With my Dad's financial support, I was able to pay my
tuition and the apartment gave me a place to study. Stan's control
game was to constantly interrupt my studying. Once I finished my
nursing degree, I kept the apartment. It had two bedrooms, so I
spent the summer furnishing it. When the school year began, the
kids and I moved in.

Your relationship with Pete is very much different. He truly loves
and respects you. But I do think that he is threatened by your
seeking a PhD and your status as an up-and-coming researcher
because of the government scholarship. I'm guessing that he needs a
little space to work out his feelings about all of this. I think he'll be
back eventually.

Only a few hours until Lauren comes back.

Veronica

To: Hansen, V
Date: Sunday, November 30
From: Stone, Charlotte P
Subject: Re: A little cheer

Hi Veronica,

You are so right about men and their control issues. I'm just waiting to see how it will all play out with the research, now that Pete and I have separated. Fortunately, Dr. Mueller is head of the project, and Dr. Fleming is co-investigator and will be my dissertation chair after I pass my qualifying exam. (She is on the SomaRx payroll and has a 50% graduate school appointment with the University. She's involved with the antidepressant research based on her expertise on health behavior.) So, Pete doesn't have any authority over me. But I imagine it could get uncomfortable with the both of us involved on the same project. Of course, I'm a student and NOT a SomaRx employee like he is.

Well, I was downstairs on the sidewalk waiting at 7:55 AM. Guess who was 15 minutes late for the arranged dropoff time? Lauren said she had a good Thanksgiving until she got the fever. She got to play with her cousins. And she thought the turkey was good.

Tomorrow should be interesting, the first time that I'll do the single mom thing, getting Lauren to school before I go to campus.

Have a good start to your workweek – Charlotte

Part Two
December

To: Stone, Charlotte P
Date: Monday, December 1
From: Strong, James Y
Subject: Query: Central College Days??

Hi!

I'm just wondering...

Are you the same Charlotte Proesser that I reconnected with at a wedding in Chicago about ten years ago? The groom was Stanton Rhodes, the bride's name escapes me. The Charlotte I'm looking for attended a summer institute at Indiana Central College the year prior to the wedding.

All the best

Jim

James Y Strong, PhD
Dean, School of Science
South Central State

To: Strong, James Y
Date: Monday, December 1
From: Stone, Charlotte P
Subject: Re: Query: Central College Days??

Nope. Not me. Quite a coincidence, though. I've never met anyone looking for someone with my maiden name, although I've occasionally run into someone looking for a Charlotte Stone. But, I never went to Indiana Central, although I was adjunct faculty there a couple of summers ago. How did you get this email address? CS

To: Stone, Charlotte P
Date: Monday, December 1
From: Strong, James Y
Subject: Re: Query: Central College Days??

Thanks, Charlotte. As far as the email address, it is amazing what our alumni relations department can do! I thought it would be worth a try to ask. You would be about the right age. However, it looks like you are in health sciences and she definitely wasn't.

All the best

Jim

James Y Strong, PhD
Dean, School of Science
South Central State

To: Strong, James Y
Date: Monday, December 1
From: Stone, Charlotte P
Subject: Re: Query: Central College Days??

Good luck with your search. If you do find the person that you are looking for, you can give her my name and email address. I've never met anyone with my maiden name before. CS

To: Hansen, Veronica
Date: Monday, December 1
From: Stone, Charlotte P
Subject: Post Turkey Day

Hey Veronica,

The weirdest thing happened today. I got an email from some guy (actually the dean of the School of Science from South Central State in Colorado) who used to know someone with my maiden name who attended Indiana Central College just south of here. Weird, huh? Anyhow, a little excitement to balance the post-holiday (and break-up) blues.

The single mom thing went okay this AM. Lauren got to school on time, just barely. I got to campus on time, just barely. Arriving 15 min. later to the parking lot means a lot less desirable parking spot. Oh well, at least I will get more exercise walking into the building.

I've explained the break-up to a few friends, and to Dr. Fleming. Three more weeks of work and classes, then I can regroup over Christmas. Lauren and I will go to my parents for a few days, and we will have some time to chill out at home, too.

I'm okay financially for now. Christmas shopping is almost done. December rent is paid. I'll get my stipend on January 2nd. When the rent rolls around on February 1, that's when things could get interesting. I'll worry about that when it happens.

I also got a call from Max, the flirty guy at Jake's Thanksgiving get-together. Like you said, I'm still married. Besides he's too young for me.

How is Van? Take care.

Charlotte

To: Stone, Charlotte P
Date: Tuesday, December 2
From: Hansen, V
Subject: Van

Hi Charlotte,

Funny you should mention Van. I haven't heard from him for a day and a half. This is highly unusual. I usually see him several times a week. On the days that I don't see him, he always emails unless he tells me in advance that he won't be able to. He has never missed a day in the time that we've been dating (over a year). But, I guess there is always the chance that this is a time when something unexpected came up in his private investigator business and he just couldn't get away. I expect him to send me some subpoenas tonight. I need to serve them tomorrow after work. I really enjoy this stuff. I even have a private investigator's card. I'm considering taking the classes to be certified in forensic nursing.

I'm sure that it was/is difficult to announce the breakup to people on campus. But I think that you are smart to do it. That keeps the rumor mongers at bay, for one thing.

I picked up the two grandsons tonight. First I met Anna and Sean at Target. Sean rode with me while I went to get Andrew from Helen's place. We went through McDonald's drive-thru to get Happy Meals. The boys were very surprised that my Thunderbird has no cup holders. When they asked me why, I told them it was because my car was too old. Sean said "Mammy, don't you know that you can get any car you want from Vehicles.com?" (He has never called me "Grandma"; it has always been "Mammy.") What a hoot! The internet even has an effect on four-year-olds. Right now they are watching TV and eating popcorn. Even though their temperaments are very different, they get along well together. On Friday, I think I will offer to keep them overnight, if their parents will let me.

Well, those emails from the Dean of Science – my, my!! Sounds pretty harmless, if you ask me. Something to make life a little less boring while you are waiting for Pete to come to his senses. It sounds like you have some things in common. If he would meet you, I'm sure that he would think that you were interesting!

Take care,

Veronica

To: Hansen, V
Date: Wednesday, December 3
From: Stone, Charlotte P
Subject: Re: Van

Hi Veronica,

I'm sure that there is a good reason why Van hasn't contacted you today. There always is when a person has such an abrupt change in behavior. I'm sure that something has come up regarding a case. You'll find out before too long and then it will all make sense.

I've been crying a lot lately. I do okay when I'm with other people, but then I lose it when I'm alone. However, once I give in and cry, I have about an hour when I can concentrate pretty well on something (after the crying spell is over – which usually lasts at least an hour). Then I get out my small data set and start playing with it. I should be getting another set of data from the biostats people at SomaRx before too long, since we've just passed the beginning of the month.

Right now, SomaRx is at the very beginning of a phase III clinical trial. This means the antidepressant drug has already been found to be safe in animals and healthy people. Now they are studying their new drug in people who actually have clinical depression. They have planned two years for recruitment of these people, probably 2000 of them. However, my dissertation won't have that many people in the sample. I'll probably stop when they get to somewhere between 500 to 800 participants.

My dissertation will look at lifestyle. Due to my nursing background, I believe that lifestyle choices (exercise, diet, work, recreation) may play a role in the response to the drug. I'll keep track of diet, exercise and sleep patterns of those who are on meds. I'll try to get information for the two weeks before they start the experimental drug (or placebo). I'm not sure if I'll be "blind" (won't know who is on the real med versus the placebo), like most of the other researchers. I guess I'm lucky to have access to this data set. SomaRx is banking on this new drug being successful. They need a successful drug right now.

Well, enough of this boring stuff. Having a private detective card sounds a lot more exciting! Take care of yourself. Try not to worry about Van, I'm sure that he is safe.

Charlotte

To: Stone, Charlotte P
Date: Wednesday, December 3
From: Hansen, V
Subject: Re: Van

Hi Charlotte,

Well, as it turns out, you were right. Van was tied up with a very tense situation. He can't tell me all of the details as of yet. But it involved an informant and a situation that didn't go as planned. He says it should be in the AM newspaper. After that, he can talk about it more. Life is never dull with him around, that is for sure! That's why I like working for him so much. Plus, like I've said before, he has many interesting stories to tell.

I admire you for trying to make sense out of all of those numbers. I don't think I could ever do research. I like patient care too much. But I do think about going into a master's in nursing program at some point. I don't think it matters how old I am, I'll know when the time is right.

Have you spoken to or had any emails from Pete? It would seem like you would need to talk to him at least once in a while. Are you doing okay? Being a little bit weepy now and then, I would think that is pretty normal. Let's try to get together for coffee before too much time goes past. Maybe we could combine that with something in the Christmas spirit.

Veronica

To: Hansen, V
Date: Thursday, December 4
From: Stone, Charlotte P
Subject: Headline!

Veronica,

I almost couldn't believe that story in this morning's newspaper. That poor girl! No wonder Van was "lost" for a while. Thank God they found her in time! What a story, even Law and Order couldn't come up with something like this. Was Van one of the cops that "busted into the garage" according to the paper? It sounds like they literally got there in the nick of time, the one guy's hands were around her neck. The fact that she didn't have to be hospitalized sounds like a miracle. I'll bet she will think twice before offering to be an informant again.

Funny you should mention Pete. Today was the first research team meeting we attended together since the breakup. I think some people probably wondered a little why I was sitting in a different place. Anyhow, after the meeting Pete came up to me and said "we should talk" soon. Just get together and go over things having to do with Lauren, and paying some of our outstanding bills. Stuff that needs to be done. While we were standing there talking, one of the other pharmacists on the project came up and invited us to a Christmas party. Evidently Sam didn't know that we were officially NOT a couple at the moment. It was awkward to say the least. Pete just looked at me rather blankly. Maybe he was trying to be respectful of my feelings and let me take the lead. I just said, "Pete and I aren't attending social functions together at the moment." Sam looked embarrassed and said, "Oh, I'm sorry" and walked away as quickly as possible. Pete looked at me and said, "What did you say that for?" I told him it was mostly because HE didn't say ANYTHING. "Well, I don't see the point of letting our private matters become public," he said. I told him that we couldn't live a charade, that I couldn't make it appear that we were still together by going to parties with him. He just looked down and clenched his jaw, then moved away from me. I was left there standing all alone – so I decided to go. I couldn't see just hanging around, feeling awkward. There will be a Christmas party for the entire research team coming up in two weeks. I may skip that one, too, even though it is pretty low-key, just held here at the plant, no alcohol involved. I'll see how I'm feeling when it rolls around. And I'll wait and see if Pete contacts me about our meeting to "talk" since that was left hanging.

Max called me yet again. Says he just wants to have coffee sometime, that I shouldn't be "afraid" of him. I don't know. Maybe I'll take him up on it, sometime. But it is still too soon. I told him to ask me again after the holidays are over.

Let me know how Van is doing after that dramatic experience. Since he's been in law enforcement for years, I imagine he has experienced a lot of this type of thing, but still...this experience must have been at least a little unusual (?)

Have a good day – Charlotte

To: Stone, Charlotte P
Date: Thursday, December 4
From: Stone, Peter E
Subject: Meeting

Hi – Sorry – I didn't mean to get angry. We do need to meet. The sooner, the better.

When and where would you be available?

Pete

To: Stone, Peter E
Date: Thursday, December 4
From: Stone, Charlotte P
Subject: Re: Meeting

Afternoons would probably work best. Maybe a late lunch at Schultz's, when the crowd starts to thin out. CS

To: Stone, Charlotte P
Date: Thursday, December 4
From: Stone, Peter E
Subject: Re: Meeting

How about tomorrow at 1:45? I'll wait until you get there before going through the line at Schultz's.

Pete

To: Stone, Peter E
Date: Thursday, December 4
From: Stone, Charlotte P
Subject: Re: Meeting

OK, see you there. CS

To: Hansen, V
Date: Friday, December 5
From: Stone, Charlotte P
Subject: Met with Pete

Hi Veronica,

Well, Pete and I met at Schultz's. We discussed some ground rules
on how we are going to proceed with informing others about our
separation. He will tell his coworkers on Monday. We will try to stay
friendly, keep each other informed about who knows what about us,
and not talk negatively about each other, especially in front of
Lauren. We will expect our parents to do the same.

There was a little bit of tension when we talked about Christmas.
Pete was trying to make me feel guilty about having Lauren over the
holiday. "SORRY," I said, "you had her over Thanksgiving." We'll be
at my parents and that trip has been planned for months. Then we
spent a couple of minutes discussing finances. I'm not as bad off as I
thought I might be, yet. However, once those issues were settled, we
had a little fun and joked around somewhat. I could hardly believe
that we were the same people that had those nasty fights.

When it was time to go, Pete pulled out my chair and helped me
with my coat. As we turned in our separate directions to go to our
cars, he put a hand on my shoulder, pulled me closer, and kissed me
on the cheek. He whispered in my ear "I do miss you." Then he
quickly walked away, before I could even answer him. I walked to
my car, got in, and the minute that the door was closed, I started to
cry. But this was not like the cries I've had over the separation
before. I did not feel sad, I felt angry! I felt like screaming, "If you
miss me why are you leaving me?" I really don't understand this at
all. Is he just trying to manipulate me? I don't think so. But I am so,

so confused. I guess it is pointless to try and make sense of Pete's behavior. It's not rational.

Let me know (if you can) what went on with Van and the informant chase that went bad.

Charlotte

To: Stone, Charlotte P
Date: Saturday, December 6
From: Hansen, V
Subject: Re: Met with Pete

Hi Charlotte,

Feelings are usually not rational – that is why they are feelings :-D! Remember our psych nurse days at St. Joseph's when we had that inservice on rational emotive therapy? What a hoot...that Albert Ellis guy on that ancient black and white educational film! He looked incapable of emoting to me.

Seriously, though (and I don't want to belittle your feelings, I'm just trying to make you laugh a little) Pete is probably just acting out his ambivalence about your situation. I doubt if he is trying to torment you. He is probably pretty tormented himself. Do you think he would go with you to counseling? It might really help a lot.

As far as the informant situation, the girl who agreed to act as the informant had just turned 20 years old. She had a short criminal history herself, but had finished out her probation for some shoplifting, I believe. Anyhow, she became aware of a plan for a robbery, so she went to the police, and agreed to have a bug put on her and act as an informant. As far as the two thugs were concerned, she was to be the lookout, and drive the getaway car. So, she met up with the two guys (who were actually a father and son) and got in their car. She thinks she's on her way to the "scene of the crime" or at least the "crime-to-be." However, the two thugs have another plan. They pull into the father's own garage, lower the door behind them and start to strangle her. The police (and Van) were in hot pursuit and broke down the garage door and not a moment too soon. The informant had lost consciousness, but was still alive and "came to" after the men stopped strangling her. There was a body bag and cement in the garage. I'd bet that girl has nightmares for a long, long time. But she is alive, and she'll probably give thanks for that fact every day of her life from now on. She will probably retire from informing, no doubt.

Well, how about coffee sometime soon? Does tomorrow afternoon work at all for you? Let me know.

Veronica

To: Hansen, V
Date: Saturday, December 6
From: Stone, Charlotte P
Subject: Coffee

Hi Veronica,

Coffee sounds wonderful!! But I do have Lauren this weekend. How does this plan sound to you? We could meet at the coffee shop just south from my church (on Illinois street) while Lauren is in Junior Church and Sunday School (beginning around 9:30). That would give us about an hour and a half. Let me know what you think.

Charlotte

To: Stone, Charlotte P
Date: Saturday, December 6
From: Hansen, V
Subject: Re: Coffee

Sounds good! I'll be at the coffee shop at 9:30.

Veronica

To: Stone, Charlotte P
Date: Monday, December 8
From: Hansen, V
Subject: New Week

Hi Charlotte,

I had fun yesterday. It was good to talk "in person." It was also a joy to see Lauren again. She is growing up fast. She reminds me of Anna when she was little.

This week is starting out on a weird note on the work scene. I have a feeling that some big changes are going to be coming down the pike. The tone of the staff meeting was very different. And, believe it or not, we were told "complaining wasn't allowed." It just feels very strange, somehow. There is some sort of agenda going on. I will just keep on doing my job. That's what they pay me to do! I admitted two patients today; one was very interesting. The holiday depression seems to be kicking in! Hope your week has started out well.

Veronica

To: Hansen, V
Date: Monday, December 8
From: Stone, Charlotte P
Subject: Re: New Week

Hi Veronica,

I also enjoyed the coffee time. I've been spending the vast majority of my time in my tiny office or in my apartment. My office doesn't even have windows – so, it was great to sit facing windows yesterday and watch the snow fall. The gingerbread latte was good, too. I felt in the holiday spirit for a while.

I am so glad that I had most of the holiday shopping done before the breakup with Pete. If I was faced with holiday shopping on top of finals and the stress of the breakup, I think I would lose it! The only shopping I have left to do is for Lauren. I guess I need to discuss that with Pete. I didn't really think of that until now. I'll give him a few days to email me. If he doesn't email me by Thursday, I will get in touch with him.

I am trying to concentrate on studying for finals. Sometimes my concentration is not so good. My plan was to do my qualifying exams in January. I had a frank talk with Dr. Fleming today about how my concentration has been affected by emotional distress and, therefore, I don't know if I will be ready. She was pretty understanding. She advised me to just play it by ear, to concentrate on finals and handing in papers on time for now. I'm to call her on January 2 or 3 and let her know if I think I can be ready for exams by the end of January. That was my original plan. I do think I can have everything for this semester done on time.

Lauren wants me to help her with her homework – so I'll close. Hang in there at work. Remember how it was at St. Joseph's? A new agenda every month. First Shared Governance – then the higher-ups decided to close our unit!

On another note... when I came in to work today, I had several spam emails in my junk folder. Nothing too unusual there, except there were a few more than usual. Then, in my inbox, there was a message from "Nobel." As in '"Nobel prize?" Anyhow, when I opened it, it said something like "If you're a woman and you want to be involved in science, think again. It will be nothing but trouble for you." That's all. It sounds threatening, but kind of impersonal, but I still don't like it. I let our technology people know; they just said that a lot of this crazy email comes into the university, and there is not a whole lot that they can do about it. They looked at where it came from, and they said it had been "spoofed"; that is, the return address wasn't real. Oh well, as long as it's not part of a trend.

There are a lot of crazy people in this world.

Take care,

Charlotte

To: Stone, Charlotte P
Date: Tuesday, December 9
From: Hansen, V
Subject: Re: New Week

Hi Charlotte,

I'm glad your professor understands how this might not be the best time for you to spend hours concentrating. Sounds like she is willing to postpone things until you can be more productive mentally. Most people do understand what it is like to go through relationship problems, how emotionally draining they can be.

We still have patients coming out of the woodwork. I think the moon may be full, plus the pre-holiday depression is really becoming evident. Believe it or not, I even had a patient call me from an inpatient unit in another hospital! She just wanted to complain about how they were treating her there, including the food. She thought I could somehow arrange it with her doctor so she could be transferred over here. Wrong! Once I realized where she was calling from, I ended the conversation as quickly as I could. I was polite though:-D!

Van has been rather quiet lately. I know he is involved with a trial about a guy accused of a horrendous crime. It sounds like the criminal was bent on killing someone on a particular day. Basically he just cruised up and down some country roads until he found someone that would be an easy target. Van heard about the "rejects." One wasn't dressed in the "right" type of clothes – meaning that they would be too hard to remove. One had two large dogs. But the third one...well, evidently she fit the bill. He raped her and then killed her in a most brutal fashion. Her children found her body when they came home from school. I hope that those kids are getting good psychiatric care; I'm sure that they need it. This guy makes no bones about his guilt. He even jokes about it. Van says he thanks the judge each time he leaves the courtroom. But he treats his lawyer like dirt. A psychiatric evaluation has been ordered. Now that is one report that I would like to read!! Since I work for Van, I may be able to do that. Right now, he has me working on his more run-of-the-mill cases, so he can concentrate on this one.

Allen and Helen are having some disagreements about the way she handles their Andrew. She just lets him throw tantrums and gives in to his demands at least half the time. So when Allen doesn't do things the same way, it just gets very difficult. I hope they can work it out, for everyone's sake. I try to stay out of it.

As far as your crazy email, yes, I would agree that it sounds somewhat threatening. I think it was good that you let the IT people know about it. But I would just delete it and definitely don't answer it. Yes, there are a lot of crazy people in the world and they probably just love to play with email, because it is so easy to be anonymous. Don't worry about it too much.

Have a good evening.

Veronica

To: Hansen, V
Date: Wednesday, December 10
From: Stone, Charlotte P
Subject: Your life!

Hi Veronica,

Your life sounds infinitely more exciting than mine right now. Wow, you get to work for someone who chases down psychopathic criminals! I sit looking at rows and columns of numbers.

Actually, I'm only being halfway facetious. Believe it or not, sometimes there is excitement in the numbers. But you just have to be patient and perseverant. One thing that I've noticed about research: no matter what the project, or what personalities are involved, there always seem to be times when you are ready to pull your hair out, or quit entirely. But if you can just muddle through that stage and keep an open mind (probably the hardest part), the message in the data becomes apparent to you.

Speaking of numbers – I just got some more data from the biostatisticians. Just eyeballing it, without running any analyses, it looks somewhat different from the data from the phase II clinical trials. There are more overweight people, for one thing. The difference is, this trial consists of subjects who are actually depressed, while the phase II trials did not; they used "healthy" people then. Well, the number of subjects right now is still small, a total of 310 so far. We'll see what happens when we get to a total of 400 people.

Still no word from Pete. He's got one more day to contact me about Christmas, or I'll have to make the move, I guess. We've got a research meeting tomorrow, too. I will let him make the first move there. In other words, if he doesn't bring up the issue with me after the meeting, I will wait until that evening and then email him about it.

Whatever you do – be careful out there!!!

Charlotte

To: Stone, Charlotte P
Date: Thursday, December 11
From: Hansen, V
Subject: Re: Your life!

Hi Charlotte,

Well, my life isn't as exciting as you probably think it is. But, I generally have plenty to keep me busy, with (almost) never a dull moment.

For example, even though this is one of the more run-of-the-mill cases, it still is interesting. Here is my "assignment" from Van: I need to call this guy and ask him to describe his ex-wife's breasts. Yes, this is the truth! There is a girl charging some guy with rape. She didn't report it for a few weeks. Of course, by that time, there is next to no physical evidence (if there ever was any). However, she does have bite marks on her left breast. She states that these occurred during the rape. However, they are extremely well-healed. I don't think they would have faded that much in just a couple of weeks. Anyhow, it is her ex-husband that I need to interview. I will do it over the phone. And I can't lead the ex-husband too much. For example, I can't say, "Did she have any bite marks on her breasts?" I may be able to ask about scars in general. I will definitely go through my list of potential questions with Van before this interview takes place. (Van thought that a woman would be better for this job.) I've read the "victim's" statement, and I can't say that I am impressed. She seems to be a person out for attention. But I'll call the "ex" and see if he can remember enough to give me a detailed description of his wife's "assets." If he can remember bite marks and identify the area where they are on her breast, it will probably be "case closed." The "accused" has a few very credible character witnesses. He admits to having sex with the accuser, but says it was consensual and that the "victim" was the one that suggested it. It is true that many rapists use a similar story, but in this guy's case – I believe him. He is cooperative and direct and establishes good eye contact. The accuser, on the other hand, has inconsistencies in her story and looks at the floor or at the ceiling a lot of the time when she is being interviewed. But that could be due to poor self-esteem or shame and the accused could be just putting on a good act. We'll see.

I really enjoy this work. I am thinking of taking some courses, maybe even getting my Master's. But – right now – I need to get to bed. Did Pete email or speak with you regarding Lauren's Christmas presents?

Sleep well,

Veronica

To: Hansen, V
Date: Thursday, December 11
From: Stone, Charlotte P
Subject: Post Research Meeting

Hi Veronica,

No, Pete did not get back with me regarding the Lauren-Christmas present issue. We had our usual research team meeting today. He more or less ignored me, but not totally. I truly think that he was trying to be civil and matter-of-fact. So I will email him when I close this email. I would like to think that he is purposefully ignoring me, but I think the truth is, he's a guy! And guys don't think about family communication issues the way women do. Christmas presents aren't his thing. Which just made me think, I wonder if he'll get me anything? I just thought of that now. I really doubt it, but maybe I'd better be prepared with something for him... just in case.

Well, when does the "breast interview" take place? You could handle something like that so much better than I could. I'm assuming that it would be over the phone? That would probably be easier for both parties. Do you know how to reach the "ex"? What happens next? I'm sure the "hearsay" wouldn't be admissible in court, or would it? I'm just totally ignorant of all of those types of legal matters. Like I said, your life is very interesting. I hope that you are keeping notes. You could write a book someday, kind of like James Herriot did about his veterinary practice, only yours would be about "things I had to do as a private investigator" or something like that.

Well, on with my task...emailing Pete!

Take care,

Charlotte

To: Stone, Peter E
Date: Thursday, December 11
From: Stone, Charlotte P
Subject: Xmas Planning for Lauren

Hi Pete,

I thought that maybe we could talk briefly about Lauren's Christmas presents. I know what she wants; you may know this too. I can drop her off at your parents' house tomorrow evening. How about if you and I go to the coffee shop on Carrollton to talk it over?

Charlotte

To: Stone, Charlotte P
Date: Thursday, December 11
From: Stone, Peter E
Subject: Re: Xmas Planning for Lauren

OK – fine. What time do you think that you will get here?

Pete

To: Stone, Peter E
Date: Thursday, December 11
From: Stone, Charlotte P
Subject: Re: Xmas Planning for Lauren

I'll be there around 5:30. See you then. Charlotte

To: Stone, Charlotte P
Date: Friday, December 12
From: Hansen, V
Subject: Boob Interview

Hi Charlotte,

Well, I interviewed the ex-husband about his ex-wife's boobs last night. Yes, it was over the phone. I started out by saying that I was a nurse, I'd worked many places including the emergency room, and there was nothing he could say that would shock or upset me. Then I explained that I was doing an investigation regarding an incident involving his ex-wife.

He was very pleasant and cooperative. I started out with some more general things…like when did they divorce, what was the reason, were they still friendly, did they have kids, etc. Then I moved to the boob questions. At first he seemed a little surprised, but he answered everything. As it turned out, as I suspected, those teeth marks are old. The ex-husband said the ex-wife had the acute injury while the two of them were married. She claimed that she "ran into a machine" at work. He said "I know a human bite when I see one." As it turns out, he is a paramedic. Actually, he said this incident was "the beginning of the end" of their marriage. He found out that she had had several affairs, even though they'd only been married three years. He has since remarried. He sounded like a very nice person. The "victim" in the case is starting to sound more and more like a borderline personality to me…creating situations where she can be the center of attention.

My job has settled down a little. All of the furtive whispering has quieted for now.

Did you email Pete? Are you going to meet with him?

Have a good afternoon – Veronica

To: Hansen, V
Date: Friday, December 12
From: Stone, Charlotte P
Subject: Re: Boob Interview

Hi Veronica,

Like I said, there's never a dull moment in your life! You could definitely write a best seller.

Yes, Pete and I are meeting this evening, as a matter of fact. I'll drop Lauren off at his parents' place and Pete and I will walk a couple of blocks to a neighborhood coffee shop and discuss the Christmas present situation. Fortunately, nothing Lauren wants should be particularly hard to find...thank goodness. I don't need any additional stress right now.

I'll write more later.

Charlotte

To: Hansen, V
Date: Friday, December 12
From: Stone, Charlotte P
Subject: Met with Pete, Part 2

Hi Veronica,

Well, Pete and I had our little "date." In some ways, that is exactly what our meeting felt like. I walked Lauren home from school. Since campus and the office are very casual on Fridays, I usually do the "casual Friday" thing and wear jeans, which is what I did today. But when Lauren and I got back to the apartment, I decided to change clothes. I put on a dress, a rather casual type of dress, but still...a dress. Then I brushed my hair and pulled it into an off-center ponytail and added a hair ornament. I put a casual jacket on over my "ensemble." The weather has been so warm, that is all that I needed in the way of a coat. I also freshened up my make-up.

Then we drove up to Broad Ripple to the Stone homestead. I went with Lauren to the door, where I was invited in while Pete got his jacket. Both of his parents were there and they were very cordial. Believe it or not, the house even smelled like apple pie! The living room was as neat as a pin, of course. Lauren and Grandpa went to the den to watch TV, and Pete and I left and walked four blocks to a quiet little coffee shop in Broad Ripple near the post office. It was getting dark then, since it was just past five, but the temperature was still unseasonably warm. It felt like spring. We got our coffees, chatted about the research a little, talked about the upcoming Christmas party, then got down to the business of the Christmas presents. I showed Pete the list that Lauren had made. We decided what items we should try to buy for her, and who would get her which one. Then Pete surprised me by saying, "You've done all of the shopping to date for Christmas. Let me handle the financial end of this. Your end of the bargain is to help me find the stuff, and the gifts can be from both of us. We can split them, she can open some early at my parents' house, and she can open some of them later at your family's Christmas celebration." I was flabbergasted. I expected some arguing, if not a downright fight. But of course, I accepted. We decided to go shopping next week. We'll bring Lauren to his parents' and we'll take off, then I'll come back and pick up Lauren.

After that we talked some more. I had a really nice time, and I think Pete did, too. For me, I think a large part of it was relief, because the fight I had prepared for never materialized. Time got away from us, and Pete said his Mom was holding supper until he got back. He asked me to stay (as did his Mom when we got to their house), but I decided against it. If they ask me next week, I probably will. But for tonight, I felt like dinner with the Stones would be too much, too soon.

When we got back to their house, however, both his parents were acting like we were two seventeen-year-olds who had just returned from a first date. After I left, they probably asked Pete, "Did you kiss her?" The situation is so strange. He's treating me nicely. Surely, he has got to get angry one of these days. His behavior doesn't make sense to me, not at all.

Tomorrow, I am going to enter into a "black hole" of sorts...devoting myself almost entirely to studying for finals and finishing up two twenty-page papers. So you may not hear too much from me this coming week. But, don't worry; I'll be in touch before too long. Hope your weekend is a good one.

Charlotte

To: Stone, Charlotte P
Date: Saturday, December 13
From: Hansen, V
Subject: The Black Hole

Hi Charlotte,

Thanks for the warning (about your "black hole voyage"). I think that women are so much better at this than men; women will generally tell you when they are going to change an established pattern of communication. Men just stop communicating without warning. They will go on a trip, be extremely busy, or whatever. But you'll never hear the explanation until later, if at all.

Anyhow, back to Pete, you know that old joke surrounding the ending of a relationship: "It's not you, it's me"? Well in this case, it is not YOU, it is Pete. I do think that Pete still loves you. But he is confused as you become more and more educated and your role continues to change. You are approaching equal footing with him on the research team. Maybe you'll lead a team before too long. Maybe before him. I know nothing about how research works, but I'm sensing that things are changing and Pete needs some space to adjust. I do think he'll be back.

I think it's a good sign that you went on your "date." And you even have a second date!

So take advantage of this time while Lauren is gone to study and write.

Van and I are going out to this little diner north of here that he likes to visit when he has business up that way. Except tomorrow there is no business; we're going up there just for fun. Now that it is getting close to the holidays, I tease him about moonlighting as a Santa. He would be a natural with his white hair and beard and his rosy cheeks. However, he doesn't think he could handle a mall setting for more than an hour. Maybe he could cover lunch breaks for the real Santa.

Anyhow, enjoy your time to concentrate!

Take care,

Veronica

To: Hansen, V
Date: Saturday, December 13
From: Stone, Charlotte P
Subject: Out of the hole

Hi Veronica,

Well, so much for the black hole...at least for a few minutes. I have admirable intentions, such as studying for an entire day, but I always fall short. I never seem able to stick to it. Even when I'm panicked over deadlines, I still have to stop and do something else for a while. Otherwise, I think I would go crazy.

Frequently, I do better going back and forth between two activities. That is what I did today for a while, I baked cookies and studied while they were in the oven. They turned out pretty well. I'll take some to my Mom and Dad's at Christmas, since I doubt if my Mom will bake anything this year. I may take some to the Stones next weekend. They will probably invite me for dinner. I could handle staying for dinner next week. I just wasn't ready for that yesterday. Anyhow, Pete's mom is a great cook and she makes some terrific desserts, but she really isn't a cookie baker. I think the Christmas cookie tradition is part of my German heritage. I can't imagine Christmas without cookies.

So right now, I'm taking a break between studying for a final and writing a paper. I got out the numbers from my dissertation data set. I have three sets of numbers. One is from the first cohort, and they have three "rounds" of data; from baseline, six months later, and six months after that. Then there is a group with two rounds of data, and a group that just enrolled, so they just have baseline. Each group has approximately the same number of participants. The people in this trial are actually depressed. So far, as a group, they are older than the people who volunteered for the phase II trial. The phase II people were NOT depressed, they were "healthy." There are also more females in the Phase III group as well.

The older I get, the more I realize that everything is about patterns. That is the way my mind works. It puts together the pieces and is always asking "What's missing? What do I need to find out to make sense of this?" But in the case of this data, the pattern is just becoming established. I'm waiting for it to reveal itself. As more people enroll, the pattern will develop. I'll have to just be patient.

Well, enough...on to paper writing!

Charlotte

To: Stone, Charlotte P
Date: Sunday, December 14
From: Hansen, V
Subject: Re: Out of the hole

Hi Charlotte,

You go girl! Data analysis, doctoral studies and cookie baking! Who says you can't do it all?

I've napped, reorganized some stuff around the house, and watched *Enchanted April* for about the fifth time. I'm out the door to pick up granddaughter Robyn. I'm going to help her with her Christmas shopping and wrapping. Some grandmother-granddaughter bonding time!

Good luck with the paper writing!!

Veronica

To: Stone, Charlotte P
Date: Sunday, December 14
From: Stone, Peter E
Subject: Friday

Hi Charlotte,

I enjoyed Friday afternoon. I do miss you. Lauren is doing well this weekend, she seems to be having fun. I'll bring her by around 7PM. Pete.

To: Stone, Peter E
Date: Tuesday, December 16
From: Stone, Charlotte P
Subject: Sorry

Hi Pete,

I'm sorry, I just now opened your email. I've been in an intense study mode for the last few days. I haven't been online, just because it interferes with the concentration. You probably thought I was kind of crazy when you bought Lauren back to the apartment. Anyhow – I enjoyed last Friday, too, and I'm looking forward to Christmas shopping for Lauren. See you tomorrow!

Charlotte

To: Hansen, V
Date: Tuesday, December 16
From: Stone, Charlotte P
Subject: Emerging from the black hole

Hi Veronica,

Well, since I haven't written for a couple of days, I've got some updating to do.

First, Pete emailed me on Sunday, but I didn't even see it until today! He just said he missed me. I still don't get this, he leaves me, he keeps repeating that he misses me, and he treats me nicely. I guess you are probably right that it IS all about HIM, but it is still very confusing for ME. I'm not prepared for this. I'm prepared for passive-aggression and barely civil communication between the two of us, at best. Well, I won't complain, this is better – at least, I think so.

On the school front, I took the one test I had and handed in the two papers. So, the semester is officially over for me. Yay! I will celebrate tonight after Lauren is in bed by watching what I call "Junk TV." Just the mindless stuff that a lot of people watch all the time, but stuff I usually don't have time to watch. I'll work in the research office tomorrow and the first part of next week. Lauren still has school for another week. Then, we'll take off for Chicago for the holiday.

I'll probably spend some time going through the data for my dissertation a little. Also, I'll make reservations to go to a research conference in late February. Dr. Fleming's grant will reimburse me for the expenses. My name is on a poster presentation of hers. I'm kind of excited to go and see what the conference is like. Pete and his parents should be able to keep Lauren.

I ran into Jake, just walking through the hospital cafeteria area today. He stopped me and asked how I was doing. He said he knew going through "a split" can be hard and he hoped I was doing okay.

He has never asked me anything personal before. I've never heard him ask about much of anything personal with anyone, come to think of it. Interesting. I told him that I was doing okay and I appreciated his thoughtfulness. I can't help but wonder if some of this info will get back to Max. I don't know what I would do if Max does call me after the holidays. I guess I will cross that bridge when I come to it.

I had neglected my university email account for a day or two. There was another "nasty-gram," this one from "Peter No one." It said "Study all you want, my pretty – it isn't going to help. Female brains can't handle complexity." So...again, threatening, or at least insulting. Again, not traceable. But it sounds like the writer knows a little about me. Knows who I am. Does he know my husband is named Peter? Probably not.

Hope your week is going well.

Charlotte

**To: Stone, Charlotte P
Date: Tuesday, December 16
From: Hansen, V
Subject: Date night?**

Hi Charlotte,

So, is tomorrow your date with Pete? At least, it sounds like a date to me! Are you going to dress up a little, like last time?

Something you maybe hadn't thought about – maybe Jake is interested in you! He just sounds like one of those very busy people that disciplines themselves to the point that they don't have much social life. And when they do have relationships, it is with people who have the same interests, partly because they do not get out of their work circles too much to meet anyone else. Anyhow, just a thought.

Van and I went to his favorite restaurant tonight, if you can call it that. He loves this old cafeteria on the north side that is family owned and run. Personally, it doesn't hold a candle to Schultz's, but since Van lives north, he won't drive that far. (Is he set in his ways, or what?) However, the place we went to near Anderson a while back is nationally known for its fried chicken, and I really enjoyed going there. Sometimes they have some entertainment as well, usually local people. It can be a lot of fun. Maybe I'll suggest going back over the holidays.

I wouldn't worry too much about the email. The "Peter" reference is probably a coincidence. After all, Peter is a common name. (And wasn't the real Peter Noone known as Herman in "Herman's Hermits"?) Also, the sender knows it is going to a university, and probably half of all the students are female. In the nursing department, it is more than 90% female, I'm sure. It is easy to see how you think it pertains specifically to you, But wouldn't most of your graduate school classmates think the same thing if they received it? Don't lose sleep over it.

I'm going to have all three of the grandkids over for a little while over the weekend, so their parents can go Christmas shopping. I got a roll of those refrigerated sugar cookies and some decorating sugar toppings, so we can do that. The kids will probably eat them all as soon as they are baked.

Maybe you and I can do lunch or dinner together at some point, after you get back from Chicago.

Veronica

To: Hansen, V
Date: Wednesday, December 17
From: Stone, Charlotte P
Subject: Re: Date Night?

Hi Veronica,

Thanks for the advice about the email. You're right of course, about how it could sound specific to a lot of people. I really hadn't thought about it that way until you pointed it out.

Well, tonight is the "date night," if you can call shopping for Christmas presents a date. I am planning what to wear. So, I feel like it IS a date. And I prepared a nice little collection of my Christmas cookies to take to Pete's mom. She actually called me and asked me to come to dinner first. As I told you, I thought she would. And I do feel up to it this week. Plus, I'll be more relaxed now that finals and papers are over.

So, I'm going to wear the aqua sweater that Pete gave me a couple of years ago. We both like it. It is comfortable, but looks good with my coloring, too. Not every color complements my reddish hair color, but this one does. I wish I had time for a haircut, but I don't before tonight. I'll do the best that I can with it. I think I will wear a skirt, too, instead of slacks or jeans.

Lauren was excited about going over to her grandparents' house again, she talked about it all through breakfast. Maybe she has the fantasy about Pete and me getting back together. I do hope that it happens. I miss Pete, too. And I still feel extremely confused about this entire experience. But I can't say that I miss the arguing and the complaints. Maybe living separately is better right now. But I can't figure out why he is so conciliatory. Maybe he feels guilty about something. Actually, that thought just popped into my head right now…I hadn't even considered it before…but it makes sense. It could be entirely why. Maybe I'll come out and ask him. But maybe not.

Well, there are a few things that I need to do to get ready before the "big night." I'll keep you posted.

More later.

Charlotte

To: Stone, Charlotte P
Date: Wednesday, December 17
From: Stone, Peter E
Subject: This evening

Hi,

I'll just plan on picking you and Lauren up after work, around 5:10 or so. That way I can drive you back to the apartment after our evening's work.

Pete

To: Stone, Peter E
Date: Wednesday, December 17
From: Stone, Charlotte P
Subject: Re: This evening

Hi Pete,

We'll be ready when you get here. You make it sound like we are going to be working on a paper together or something. Hopefully, we'll have some fun, too.

Charlotte

To: Hansen, V
Date: Thursday, December 18
From: Stone, Charlotte P
Subject: Last night

Hi Veronica,

Well, last night was very interesting. And somewhat disappointing. But the disappointment is probably my fault. I should have known better than to think of it as a date.

First of all, I think the reason that both Pete and I were surprised by last weekend is that we were both pretty nervous about it and each of us expected the other to be at least somewhat adversarial. When that didn't happen, we both felt relieved. Maybe even happy, in a way. I probably read too much into that sense of relief.

My expectations regarding last night may have been way, way too high. Pete picked us up prior to "the evening's work" as he put it. Hardly sounds romantic, or even friendly. Sounds very business-like. He was cordial, but not overly friendly when he picked us up. Lauren gave him a big hug that he wasn't very enthusiastic about, at least it didn't look like it. He has never been much of a hugger, though.

When we got to Pete's parents' house, his mom had dinner almost on the table and we sat down to eat pretty quickly (I guess so Pete and I could get to our work.) The food was good, and the conversation was pretty comfortable. Then Lauren asked, "Daddy, are you ever going to come back to live with us?" It got quiet very quickly. I didn't know if I should say something or not. Finally, Pete said, "I can't answer that right now, Lauren." Lauren's lower lip stuck out and then she started to cry. I excused the two of us from the table and went into the hallway to talk to her. I explained that Daddy really couldn't answer that question right now because he was trying to figure things out for himself. Hopefully, it wouldn't take too long, but we should let him tell us, not ask questions about it. I reassured her that Daddy did love her, so that made Lauren somewhat happier. She was able to come back to the table and eat her dinner without any other incidents. The conversation picked up again; but, as you can imagine, it was pretty guarded.

Pete and I skipped dessert so we could get to our task and drove to the Toys R Us on the north side. It was crowded, of course. We decided to split the list and find what we could individually to save time. Then, if anything was still left, something that couldn't be located, we'd look for it together.

We were lucky in that we found everything on the list. A lot of the things that Lauren wants are not the popular, fad toys, which definitely helps. She still likes a lot of fantasy, dress-up, costume-type things. I also got her some play makeup as a stocking stuffer. She also likes science toys, and Pete also got her a couple of extra gadgets in that category to add to her stocking. What a combo –

girly stuff and science gadgets. Maybe she'll grow up to be like her mom!

We decided on the way back to the Stones' that we would leave the presents in the trunk of Pete's car for now, and Pete would drop them off sometime later during the week, when Lauren was asleep. We sat in the driveway in the parked car for a few minutes. Pete said he was sorry for the distress he was causing us. I said it was really hard for a 7-year-old to make sense of this situation, and he said it was hard on him, too. I asked him if he was hiding anything from me in the last few months. He looked really, really surprised. He said, "No, there isn't anyone else, if that is what you mean." I said I hadn't thought that there was, but the idea had occurred to me just recently. Then he said that he was thinking and reading a lot and trying to figure himself out. I asked him if he would be willing to go to marriage counseling. Once again, he looked very surprised. He said that he would need to think about that. So we'll see.

We went in and Lauren put her coat on for the trip home. Pete's mom had helped her make caramel corn while we were gone and it smelled wonderful. Grandma had packaged some up for us to take home. Lauren fell asleep in the car, and Pete helped me carry her up to the apartment. We got her coat off and laid her down on the bed. We both knew that she would wake up before she fell asleep "for good." Even as a baby, she never slept well in clothes. She would always wake up and fuss until she was in something comfortable.

Pete said, "Hey, I'll be in touch." I said "OK." It was a little awkward. Then he left.

So that was the night. Confusing, sometimes uncomfortable, but productive. We got our "work" done. Pete probably regards it as successful. I am somewhat disappointed. But I guess my fantasy of getting back together quickly and relatively painlessly was just that – a fantasy. On the plus side, we were civil and friendly toward each other and worked together on a common task. I don't think it is a hopeless situation.

This is the longest email that I have written in a long, long time. You can tell that the semester is over for me! Take care.

Charlotte

To: Stone, Charlotte P
Date: Thursday, December 18
From: Hansen, V
Subject: Re: Date Night?

Hi Charlotte,

I continue to be impressed by how well that you are handling all of this. Things didn't go as you had hoped, but you still handled it with grace and maturity.

Van has been in a weird mood. His emails have been cryptic and brief. The case of the psychopathic killer could be getting to him, in one way or another. He has dealt with all types of criminals, so I don't think that is it. It must be pressure from the lawyers or something else related to the "business" side of the case. The accused is one messed up young man. He almost seems like the "Psycho" type. That is, his real conflict is with his mother. I do know that he had a terrible childhood. He has drawn some graphic and violent pictures of his mother and their family life when he was a child. One time, when his mother came to a pre-trial hearing, he threw a pencil at her and it hit her in the middle of the forehead. If he was aiming for just between the eyes, he came awfully close. At the conclusions of everything in the courtroom, he always looks right at the judge and says, "Thank you, your Honor." I'm sure it is somewhat stressful working on a case with someone who is both violent, and crazy to some degree. Plus it doesn't seem appropriate to be working on this type of thing so close to Christmas. It will go to the jury close to the holidays.

I really don't know what to get for Van for Christmas this year. I am really, really stuck for an idea. I'll sleep on it, maybe I'll come up with something. What did you decide to do about Pete's gift?
I need to go to sleep; I need to go to work early in the AM. I'll be up at 4:45. It comes around awfully fast.

Take care and hang in there – Veronica

To: Hansen, V
Date: Saturday, December 20
From: Stone, Charlotte P
Subject: Re: Date night?

Hi Veronica,

Thanks for all of the compliments, but I really don't think I'm so mature. I just don't know what else I could do about the situation.

I'll bet you're right about Van. That case must be really getting to him, so I'd just ignore the curt behavior as it will probably disappear when the case is over. Let me know what you decide about his Christmas gift. I'm still debating about Pete's.

Charlotte

To: Stone, Charlotte P
Date: Sunday, December 21
From: Hansen, V
Subject: The Perfect Gift

Hi Charlotte,

I think I thought of the perfect gift for Van. Not that it will help you with Pete's; at least, I don't think so. Van has a thing about the county courthouses in Indiana, and has photographed about half of them. He has a special album for these photos, I have seen it once. If his business takes him to or near a courthouse he hasn't photographed yet, he will make it a point to get a few photos to add to his collection.

Anyhow, I found a book that has all of the Indiana courthouses in it, so I think that I will get that for him. I think he will like it, and he may be motivated to make special trips to add to his own collection. I feel relieved, now that I've gotten this taken care of. I found it today when I went to the bookstore. They also had a lot of other historical books about Indiana.

I also got Van some of the sandalwood scented soap that he likes and a restaurant gift card to the fried chicken place in Anderson. So, I think that I'm set. Now I just have a few items for the grandkids, I think I have my own kids pretty much taken care of. It is a big relief to have that done. I think you were smart to get the bulk of your Christmas shopping done early.

By the way, whatever happened to the SomaRx Christmas party? I haven't heard you mention it for a while.

There's a sentimental Christmas movie on HBO Tonight, and I am in the mood for that, so I think I'll watch it in bed. I hope that your week goes smoothly. Is Lauren in school this week?

Take care – Veronica

To: Hansen, V
Date: Monday, December 22
From: Stone, Charlotte P
Subject: Guess What??

Hi Veronica,

I was going to email you again last night, but...Jake called! He just wanted to chat (I guess). We talked for almost an hour, about research, about plans for the holidays, about our families. But not about the two of us, or either one of us, or about Pete. He knows Pete vaguely, but they have never been involved on any of the same projects. Jake has more of a public health focus, as opposed to pharmaceutical research background. He also is quite a bit younger than I am. Now that I think about it, I wonder if he was calling to get info for his friend, Max, who promised to call me after the holidays. Hmmm. Well, the conversation was kind of fun, but I really didn't know what the agenda was. I guess I still don't.

Funny you should ask about the SomaRx Christmas party. It was canceled – or I guess I should say, postponed. The person who usually does the bulk of the work in planning it is on maternity leave and I guess no one else thought that they could handle it. SO, they decided to wait until January. They rationalized it by saying that most people have a lot of parties to attend in December, so this would make one less at that busy time of year, and we would have one in January to look forward to. Weird, huh? Oh well, at least I don't have to make a decision about attending right away.

I need to go to the office for a few hours today. I'll leave early though. Lauren has an invitation to play at a friend's house, and I'll pick her up after I'm done.

Hope your workday is going well.

Charlotte

To: Stone, Charlotte P
Date: Monday, December 22
From: Hansen, V
Subject: Re: Guess What??

Hi Charlotte,

My workday is going okay. I'm jealous that you get a little "unstructured time" during this hectic season.

My gut-level impression is that JAKE is interested in you. But, I've said that before. He also sounds like a nice guy, very concerned, and also willing to take things at a slow pace. Who cares if he is younger than you! Pete had better be careful!

We're pretty busy today. More later.

Veronica

To: Hansen, V
Date: Monday, December 22
From: Stone, Charlotte P
Subject: Re: Guess What??

Hi Veronica,

Well, I don't know about your Jake theory. He's just a nice guy, I think. And I do value him as a friend.

Yes, Lauren has school the first part of the week, so I get a little break. Pete is going to come over tonight after she is asleep and we will wrap her presents. I'm not really looking forward to that. She's a sound sleeper, luckily, but if she does wake up, I'm not worried about her seeing the presents so much as I am worried about her seeing Pete there. If that happens, it could get her fantasies going about us getting back together. It is pretty obvious that she thinks a lot along those lines. So, even though it feels sneaky, having Pete come over after she's asleep is the best way. I'll call him on his cell.

I plan to use this opportunity to ask him a few things. Like...does he ever see us getting back together? At least, the possibility of us getting back together? If not, should I being seeing other people? I've been getting subtle clues already that some guys might be interested. All it takes is the nod from me. Personally, I would rather that Pete and I work out our differences and reunite. I don't have a strong interest in anyone else right now. But I am not into living a nun's existence either. So I think I have the right to know what he is thinking along those lines. Or at least, I need to let him know that I cannot wait forever. Maybe that is his control game – one of them. He knows I don't approve of cheating. So, by moving out, he may know that he is denying me any kind of sex life. But I won't put up with that for long. I'm not the pawn for any game-playing. But I will be honest with him. I'll let him know when, and if, I start dating. And maybe it will start with Max, for coffee, in January. We'll see if he follows up after the holidays.

Back to work. Look for the update later!!! Charlotte

To: Stone, Charlotte P
Date: Monday, December 22
From: Hansen, V
Subject: Re: Guess What??

Hi Charlotte,

You will ask Pete some good questions. You have the right to know how you stand with him.

We're "crazy-busy" lately at work. I don't know if there is a full moon or if it is the holiday season, but we'll have potential patients coming out of the woodwork tomorrow...I guarantee it! Good luck tonight!

Veronica

To: Hansen, V
Date: Monday, December 22
From: Stone, Charlotte P
Subject: Post Report

Hi Veronica,

Well, well, well. Last night was very interesting. Very, very interesting.

First, as far as the task at hand, wrapping Lauren's gifts – we got it done. Lauren did wake up once, but fortunately I heard her stirring and got her a drink of water. She quickly went back to sleep and she was unaware that Pete was there.

I did come out and ask Pete (after the wrapping was done and the packages were out of sight) what his plans were for the future. I asked him if he saw us getting back together.

He looked at me like I was crazy and said he had no plans. That was why he moved out. He needed time and space apart from me to think it through. So, I asked what he had been thinking, since he had been out of the apartment for a few weeks now. He said it hadn't been long enough to know. So I asked him how long it would take. He said, "Are you giving me some kind of ultimatum here?" I said no, but I wanted to know what I should be doing with MY life. That I could only put it "on hold" for so long. That (evidently) people were interested in me. Should I be pursuing relationships? That is what I wanted to know. He said, "That does sound like an ultimatum." Like I was telling him to hurry up and decide – or else! I tried to explain myself again...then he interrupted. He started to get really angry, but did manage to keep his voice at a whisper. At one point, he used the word "bed-hopping." Something like he thought I was getting ready to go bed-hopping, or something like that. I said I didn't believe in doing things behind people's backs. What I really needed to know was: Is it over? Between you and me – is it over? And he said he couldn't say. So I said, "Okay. Let's let it rest for now, until after the holidays, at least." He said, "Okay" and got up and left. He said he would email me about Lauren's last visit with him and his family before the holidays. Hmm...Pete's family. That used to include me.

So, that was the evening, in a nutshell. I feel confused, but kind of at peace. Because, at least I was able to ask what I wanted to ask and not back down. The answer (or lack of it) was kind of disturbing, but it was more or less what I expected. And now Pete knows that I won't wait forever, and he can't keep me captive as some type of pawn to play with in his life. As I write this, I'm feeling better and better. It was my way of putting my foot down.

The snow is falling outside. It looks so Christmas-y. I think I will put on the kettle and have a cup of herbal tea before bed.

Take care.

Charlotte

To: Stone, Charlotte P
Date: Monday, December 22
From: Hansen, V
Subject: Re: Post Report

Hi Charlotte,

Well, "bed-hopping" does sound like a cruel accusation. But I'm going to play devil's advocate here. You've only been separated for three weeks or so, right? Pete probably is just trying to figure himself out. Plus, it is the holiday season, there are a lot of distractions, a lot of things going on that take time and energy away from this very difficult task of figuring out his feelings. On the plus side, he's been very decent (I think) in helping with Lauren's

Christmas, etc. Of course, he should be helping out – but in my line of work I've seen so many cases where that doesn't happen. And comparing Pete's behavior with Stan's...well, there is no comparison.

Then you demand that Pete let you know what his plans are. He may have felt totally blindsided.

Now, before you start hating me, I do see your side, too. You're lonely, you may feel abandoned. Some guys, some very nice men, as a matter of fact, are giving you hints that they are interested. So, it is not unusual to want to know where you stand.

This situation cries out for marital counseling, in my not-so-expert opinion.

Are you getting ready to go to your parents'? Maybe a change of locale, and pace, will do you a world of good. Try to relax and enjoy letting your family take care of the holiday hustle and bustle as much as you can. Besides being good for you, it will let them feel like they are able to help you through this difficult time.

Veronica

To: Hansen, V
Date: Tuesday, December 23
From: Stone, Charlotte P
Subject: No worries

Hi Veronica,

Don't worry, I don't hate you! I had some of the same ideas about Pete and his feelings as you do (and I do consider you an expert, by the way). I can't deny that I'm angry with him. Maybe I want to punish him. I do feel very, very deserted and abandoned. Also, my 40th birthday is coming up in January. If he is going to leave me ultimately, I'd just as soon have the "heads up" regarding that.

But I can only think about that kind of stuff for so long. Christmas is just around the corner. I was at the bagel shop the other day and bought a pound of their holiday coffee. An unnecessary extravagance, I know. I'm rationalizing by calling it a Christmas present to myself.

Speaking of Christmas presents, I decided to get my hair cut, finally! I've needed it for a while. Fortunately, I've been able to get by without one, by using different hair ornaments and pulling it back. But I'm going to splurge today and get it done while Lauren is still in school. Today is her last day until after New Year's.

So, I'll go and see my friend Alejandro. Getting a haircut at his salon is truly an adventure, but also a luxury. First, he washes and conditions your hair with many good-smelling products. Secondly, he is extremely talented and cuts your hair about one strand at a time (at least it seems that way). It always looks great! Thirdly, he takes his time. He is a good listener – which kind of amazes me since he is a bachelor and probably is bored to death with my domestic tales. But he has very interesting tales to tell. He loves the outdoors and geology. So...a haircut...my treat to myself!! Plus, I'm going to go a little shorter, I need a new image.

Then I'll come home and do a little packing up for the trip north. I just hope that the weather holds, I don't want to drive north in snow or ice. Watch for an update!

Charlotte

To: Hansen, V
Date: Tuesday, December 23
From: Stone, Charlotte P
Subject: Update (post-cut)

Hi Veronica,

Well, I'm back from my adventurous trip to Alejandro's salon. I do look different.

First, by my standards, I got a lot of length cut off, probably about four inches. It is now kind of a long bob. Secondly, Alejandro's appointment following mine canceled. By this time I think he was feeling sorry for me – because I told him about Pete. I didn't intend to, but it kind of slipped out when he asked how my family was doing. So he put in a few, very few highlights around my face since he had some extra time. As he said, they are subtle enough that I can just let them grow out with looking tacky. Or, if I want to, I can add more highlights later. But, he says they really look great with my red-blond hair. He also said the highlights were his Christmas present to me. He even gave me a little hug as I left. I think it was a "Merry Christmas" thing. I've been going to him for over four years now, and he's never done that before. I think it was his way of saying that he's in my corner. He also told me a few stories about tough times in his family around the holidays, like the time one of his brothers was missing on Christmas and wasn't located until late in the evening of the 25th.

So there's a "new me." Pete probably won't see my new image until after the holidays – unless he invites me in when I pick up Lauren tonight. Pete is going to take her home with him after work and she'll open her presents from Grandma and Grandpa Stone and have dinner with them. I'll use the time to do some laundry before packing for the trip north.

Charlotte

To: Stone, Charlotte P
Date: Tuesday, December 23
From: Hansen, V
Subject: Courage

Hi Charlotte,

What a brave woman! I'll be anxious to see the new look.

I may get the number of Alejandro's salon from you. Maybe it is time that I stop cutting my own hair! I've been a little afraid to go to a salon after some bad experiences. But that was years ago. When you said that Alejandro cuts your hair "one strand at a time" that got me thinking…maybe this is a hair stylist I can trust.

Helen is throwing her typical Xmas histrionics. It seems that we go through this every year – even before the divorce – but it is worse since. She gets "first pick" of days to have Christmas this year, but she keeps changing the date. Obviously a little control game that she delights in torturing Allen with. It is almost as bad as the low cut sweaters she wears. I think that I told you that she had a boob job, right?? It seems like every time Allen comes to pick up the kids, she had on a low cut sweater and does the little bending over routine. I've actually witnessed this a couple of times. Allen tells me about the others.

Well, the countdown to Christmas in on – I'm pretty much done with the shopping. I've ordered a standing rib roast for the gang from the butcher shop on Illinois Street. We've got two potential dates picked out to celebrate – one will be chosen when Helen makes up her mind.

When exactly do you leave for your parents and when do you come back?

Stay warm! A cold front is supposedly on the way. How is the heat working in your apartment?

Veronica

To: Stone, Charlotte P
Date: Tuesday, December 23
From: Oberon
Subject: See below

I have seen you. You are my Titania. You will try to resist me, but I will win you over.

Oberon

To: Hansen, V
Date: Tuesday, December 23
From: Stone, Charlotte P
Subject: Re: Courage

Hi Veronica,

Okay. I'm trying not to get hysterical here. But now – I'm getting weird emails in my personal account. This one sounds like it is from a real creep. Says I am his "Titania," and he will win me over. It is signed, "Oberon." Like I said, I'm trying not to get hysterical – but this really, really bothers me. And scares me a little. I have NEVER had this kind of thing in my personal email. NEVER. I sent it to my internet service provider. Do you think that I should do anything else?

I guess I'm glad that we're leaving town. Lauren and I will leave tomorrow and we'll be back on the 3rd, give or take a day. We're not firmly committed to the day that we'll be leaving my parents' place. But I want to be back a couple of days before Lauren has to head back to school.

I got down the huge suitcase we used to use for family get-away weekends. It was big enough for all three of us to use and then we'd just have one bag to worry about. This time it will hold most of the clothes Lauren and I will need for a week, plus some of the Xmas gifts. Lauren wants to take her PJs in her little pink backpack, and I'll need one large shopping bag for the rest of the Xmas gifts and cookies, but that's about it.

Lauren will be at the Stones' for 2 or 3 hours this evening. Pete's parents will give her their gifts tonight, but I bet I won't see Pete. I just have the feeling that he won't make any effort to see me. I will wait at the apartment entrance with Lauren after school and just send her out to the car when he arrives. And I bet he doesn't make an appearance when I come by to pick her up.

Yes, I really like the haircut and the few highlights around my face. I've never been disappointed in one of Alejandro's haircuts yet. I do think that you can trust him. Maybe it IS time for you to stop cutting your own hair!!

Well, time to start the packing. I'm getting out of town soon. Like you said, the countdown is on.

Charlotte

To: Stone, Charlotte P
Date: Tuesday, December 23
From: Hansen, V
Subject: Don't Bet on It!

Hi Charlotte,

I wouldn't bet on Pete avoiding you. I think he'll try to see and talk to you tonight. Do you want to bet a latte at Starbucks after the holidays?

And don't worry too much about the email thing. It does sound weird, though, and reporting it was the wise thing to do.

Veronica

To: Hansen, V
Date: Tuesday, December 23
From: Stone, Charlotte P
Subject: Re: Don't Bet on It!

You're on!! (Re: the bet for a latte.) Watch for the breaking news...

Charlotte

To: Hansen, V
Date: Tuesday, December 23
From: Stone, Charlotte P
Subject: News: Don't Bet...

Hi Veronica,

OK, you win! This has been an interesting evening.

Pete picked Lauren up on his way home from work. I waited downstairs with her until he pulled up in the loading area. Lauren was ready and looking forward to the evening, partly because she would get to open presents. She ran out to the car when he pulled up, I waved at both of them, and that was that! I went upstairs, nuked a frozen dinner, and looked at the data again. Actually, this was a larger data set, because I just added the newest subjects that have completed the baseline data collection. And of course, more have finished some of the follow-up data collections points as well.

Anyhow, these subjects are definitely different from those in the Phase II trial. Their responses to the medication appear to be different. As I get more subjects, the difference becomes more and more obvious. (I was hoping the difference would disappear as we got more people in the study.) I wasn't going to take any work home with me, but I think that I will take this data to look at between Christmas and the New Year. I need to try and figure out why the differences are occurring. Anyhow, I got quite engrossed in the numbers. Thank goodness, I had set the alarm so I didn't miss getting over to the Stone house on time. I took a minute (yes, really, under a minute) to put on a little blush, eye shadow, and lipstick. After all, I had the new haircut, so why waste it, just in case...

Well, I went to the door, and Pete answered. I could hear Lauren laughing at something on TV in the den. Pete said, "Lauren was telling me that you looked like you went for a makeover today. I thought I'd better see for myself." So I said, "What do you think?" And he said, "I think you are looking good." He was smiling. So I don't think he was thinking that I was getting ready to go "bed-hopping." So I said, "I do miss you." And this time I kissed HIS cheek. But I didn't walk away. Then I gave him his Christmas card – and I also gave him a gift card to Starbucks He is addicted to mocha lattes. (Not the best gift I could think of, but I was in a hurry.) He gave me a card, too, and a single rose in a vase with a red ribbon and holly sprig. There was a card attached that said "Enjoy this rose now, another will be awaiting your return." By this time, Lauren was in the entry way, getting her coat and mittens on. Pete's parents gave me a little gift wrapped in multicolored paper with a silver ribbon. "For under your tree," they said. I gave them the little gifts I'd bought three months ago and a tin of the cookies that I had baked while studying. We said the obligatory "Merry Christmases." And then Lauren and I left. As I was helping Lauren into the car, Pete opened the door and yelled, "Drive carefully, you two!" I said we would, and I'd call or email to let him know when we arrived.

Oh, yes. I also told him about the weird emails, and like you, he said not to worry. He says that kind of thing happens all of the time at SomaRx. Also, he pointed out that I had a little article published in an online publication, and both my email addresses were listed as ways to contact me. So both addresses were probably harvested by spammers...they do things like that. Now that I know why it is happening, I'm a lot less worried.

So, all in all, a rather nice conclusion to the year in Indianapolis... considering the circumstances anyway. Tomorrow...Chicago or bust!!

Take care,

Charlotte

To: Stone, Charlotte P
Date: Tuesday, December 23
From: Hansen, V
Subject: Be safe!

Hi Charlotte,

I will echo Pete's sentiments. Drive carefully, you two! May you have a peaceful and meaningful Christmas. Let me know when you get back.

Veronica

To: Hansen, V
Date: Wednesday, December 24
From: Stone, Charlotte P
Subject: Re: Be safe!

Hi Veronica –

We will (drive carefully and be safe!). You do the same (have a great Christmas). I hope the standing rib roast turns out picture-perfect, and that you and your kids and grandkids have your best Christmas ever.

I'll probably email you once from my parents' place. I'll let you know when we get back.

Charlotte

To: Stone, Peter E
Date: Wednesday, December 24
From: Stone, Charlotte P
Subject: Safe Arrival

Hi Pete,

Lauren and I arrived in Chicago without much difficulty. It snowed a little near the Rensselaer exit, but otherwise the roads were clear. Lauren slept part of the way, and played with her recent Christmas gifts the rest of the time. Now we're safe in my parents' Hyde Park condo. My mom seems pretty much the same as she did in September, cognitively speaking. She is cheerful and makes the same jokes about her memory.

By the way, we are going to go up to the lake house in Wisconsin for a couple of days between Christmas and New Year's (December 28, 29, 30). This was my parents' idea, but I guess it should be fun. I have my cell phone with me, of course, so I should be able to monitor calls and email. I'll keep you posted regarding our return to Indy.

Have a good Christmas. I'll miss you.

Charlotte

To: Hansen, V
Date: Saturday, December 27
From: Stone, Charlotte P
Subject: Post-Holiday

Hi Veronica,

I hope your Christmas went well, that is, if you celebrated it by now. I guess I don't know what date you actually settled on to have your family celebration…Helen was still trying to make up her mind. Ours was okay. I helped my mom with the shopping (for the ingredients for Christmas dinner) and then helped her prepare it. My aunt and uncle and their youngest daughter were here also. It was a relaxed time. After dinner we played board games and Yahtzee and laughed over family events in the past. Lauren enjoyed opening gifts for the second time, and of course Santa came here as well. We sent him a letter from Indy telling him where she would be!

Every once in a while my mom will ask, "Where's Pete?" So I have to go through the whole story each time. I don't know if that is good therapy for me or not. On the 28th we leave for the lake house east of Oostburg, Wisconsin. It's very close to the Lake Michigan shore. The trip should be a different experience, I haven't been there in the winter since junior high. I may be able to email from there…we'll see.

Take care,

Charlotte

To: Hansen, V
Date: Sunday, December 28
From: Stone, Charlotte P
Subject: East of Oostburg

Hi Veronica,

It is now about 1:00 AM. I feel like I have this place all to myself. The fireplace is down to its last embers. Lauren and my parents are asleep, I can hear my mother snoring softly.

We didn't have any trouble getting through the Chicago traffic this morning since it was Saturday. We stopped in Milwaukee for lunch at one of their great German restaurants, and then the rest of the trip went by quickly. It was kind of misty when we arrived here in the mid afternoon. The pine trees looked pretty cool in the mist, and there were a few redbirds flitting around, very picturesque. There is some snow on the ground, but it is kind of "crunchy," like the top layer has melted and then frozen.

This is an old cottage close to the shore of Lake Michigan. There is an old barn on the property, too, that was used as an icehouse before refrigeration. Ice was cut from the lake in the winter and covered in sawdust. Believe it or not, some of it is still there. My parents had most of the interior walls removed in the cabin when they bought it. It's now one big open room with a sleeping loft. I'm the only one in the downstairs area now. I just made myself a cup of instant decaf and I'm mulling over these numbers from the study. I've done a little manipulating of the data and I think I've found at least one reason for the difference in the data from the earlier trial. I split the subjects by age, looking at those over 45 years old and those younger. I also split them by sex. In the men, so far, there weren't any major differences in the older versus the younger ones. But in the women, the older women had a lot less improvement in their depressive symptoms when contrasted with the younger ones. Furthermore, they gained significantly more weight than the younger women and all of the men. I don't know what this means exactly. But if this trend continues, it means the new drug should not be prescribed for the older women because (a) it doesn't look like it works and (b) it seems to have at least one bad side effect. Of course, we're still in the early stages of the trial, and we still only have a relatively small number of subjects. But when I get back, I'd better call this to someone's attention. Maybe I'll discuss it with Pete first. I'm glad I brought the data with me. Here at night, with everyone else asleep – it's the perfect place to concentrate.

I assume that your Christmas celebration has taken place by now. Let me know how things are going. Do you have to work the day of New Year's Eve? Do you have any exciting plans?

I really miss Pete tonight. I miss his physical presence, and I'm not talking about sex – this is something different. I miss his being here, with me. Maybe I'll email him soon.

Take care,

Charlotte

To: Stone, Peter E
Date: Sunday, December 28
From: Stone, Charlotte P
Subject: Miss You

Hi Pete,

I'm at the Oostburg cabin now, and my parents and Lauren are asleep in the loft. It is so quiet. I've been looking at the numbers that I'll be using for my dissertation. It has been a productive evening, but I'll discuss that part with you later.

I'm writing because I miss you...a lot. I wish you were here with me right now. This place is different in the winter, and I think you would like it. It is beautiful, and quiet. Right now a light snow is falling, I can see it in the lamppost of the property south of this place.

I'll email you when I am back in Indy. I hope that you had a good Christmas. Lauren enjoyed her presents, we picked out the right items, evidently!

Love,

Charlotte

To: Stone, Charlotte P
Date: Sunday, December 28
From: Hansen, V
Subject: Almost new year

Hi Charlotte,

The cabin on the lake sounds wonderful. Do your parents ever rent it out?

My Christmas was good, kind of chaotic, but good. We ended up celebrating yesterday. Because it was a Saturday, I was off, and had plenty of time to prepare the dinner. I know I wouldn't have had to do anything that elaborate, but I wanted to. The standing rib roast turned out great! I also made Yorkshire pudding to go with it, and a trifle for dessert, which was easy to do. The kids loved that part.

The gift opening was frenzied. The boys just have no patience, but it was fun to watch. But the best part was having everyone together. I am more than willing to have our family celebration on a day other than the 25th, as long as we can all be here.

I helped out at work getting gifts together for the inpatients that had nowhere else to go over the holiday. I knew something about the ones that I did the intake assessments for, so I tried to pick out gifts that they would like (the hospital donates unsold items from their gift shop). One person wrote out a thank you note that I received on the 26th. Sometimes I am blown away by the small gesture you can regard as almost insignificant, yet it is so meaningful to someone else. Kind of like it says in the New Testament: "If you have done it to the least of these..." Now I'm getting weepy.

I did go to Mass this AM, and it was beautiful. I also went to midnight Mass on Christmas Eve and saw several people I knew there – all single people in my age group. We decided we would try and get together after the holidays...we'll see if it happens. Maybe I'll take the lead on getting everyone together.

Van is busy...a new murder case to work on! For some people, the holidays bring out their worst side, unfortunately. More on this later.

It is late, and I have to work tomorrow. So far, I have no New Year's Eve plans, but I imagine that Van and I will do something. (I do have to work during the day on the 31st.) Darn!

Enjoy the cabin and the chance to have some peace and quiet.

Veronica

To: Stone, Charlotte P
Date: Monday, December 30
From: Stone, Peter E
Subject: Re: Miss you

Hi Charlotte,

I miss you, too. I missed seeing Lauren under the tree on Christmas morning. My Mom's sister and her new boyfriend were here. It was awkward sometimes. Late in the afternoon, I went out with George (SomaRx pharmacist from the UK) since he couldn't get home over the holiday.

I hope to see you soon.

Pete

To: Hansen, V
Date: Monday, December 30
From: Stone, Charlotte P
Subject: Re: Almost new year

Hi Veronica,

I heard from Pete! A pretty short email, but still...from him, that's good. And he did say he missed me, and Lauren, of course. He is probably lonely, at least a little bit, maybe a lot. Christmas is a family time of year.

Lauren and I went out and walked on the beach today. That is a different experience in the dead of winter!! But we had fun. My Mom made gingerbread and hot cocoa for us when we came in. She seems to enjoy being in the kitchen and putting together some tasty items for us (as long as they come from a packaged mix). We played Yahtzee for a while after that. Tonight some relatives are coming over for bratwurst and beer. I will parboil the bratwurst in some of the beer before they arrive. Then we'll finish cooking the brats over the fire. These relatives are my Dad's second cousin and his wife. They ran a dairy farm in this area forever, but now they have retired and live in Oostburg. My Dad is listening to this polka radio station they have up here. It's polka, 24 hours a day! Only in Wisconsin! I'm not tired of it...yet!

Hopefully your work week is a little more fun than usual!

Take care,

Charlotte

To: Stone, Charlotte P
Date: Wednesday, December 31
From: Hansen, V
Subject: Out with the old...

Hi Charlotte,

Well, work is a little more fun than usual. We didn't have any admissions today. The one we had on the books did not show up. I caught up on some paper work, then spent some time with Lara in Utilization Review in order to learn something about pre-authorizing admissions. My boss thought that it would be helpful for me to learn about that end of the business; figuring out each insurance provider's rules about what healthcare is covered for each insurance plan that we take here. It seems complicated. But like any set of rules, the more that you work with them, the easier it gets.

I'm excited about tonight. Van is picking me up around 8:00. He has made reservations somewhere. He's keeping the exact location secret. But he did tell me to bring a suitcase! And he said I should dress up...something he has never said to me before. We'll see what happens. I like surprises. We've talked a lot, but we haven't seen each other face-to-face since the 23rd. We had our own family celebrations, and he has been very busy with his work.

Wow, polka, brats, beer – it could only be Wisconsin. Enjoy!

Veronica

Part Three
January

To: Hansen, V
Date: Friday, January 2
From: Stone, Charlotte P
Subject: Back home in Indiana

Hi Veronica,

Well, we're back. We were in Chicago last night, after driving back from the cottage during the afternoon. It was very pleasant driving back from Oostburg. The sun was shining almost all of the way. Lauren and I spent one more night with my parents at their condo. We got up fairly early and went to one of our old Hyde Park haunts for breakfast before heading back. Pete and I used to come to the same place for coffee when we were dating. It is where I unloaded my soul to him because of the trauma in the NICU with all of those premature babies looking at me. We met on the University of Chicago campus when I was a newly graduated RN faced with a kind of culture shock. He was a newly graduated Doctor of Pharmacy working on a research project. It had to do with investigating the effects of a well-known drug on neonates. He would come around to the Intensive Care Nursery to get blood samples at all hours of the night. He kept track of when all of the babies were given their doses, and timed his data collection accordingly. He was, and is, very dedicated to doing the process right. That was one of the things that attracted me to him.

Anyhow, every once in a while, we would go to this place (called the Medici) for coffee, eggs, and toast after a night in the Intensive Care

Nursery. Neither one of us looked too good after being up all night. Mainly we talked about the varying degrees of shock we had at what we saw there. So many of the babies born at that time were addicted to something – usually crack, heroin, methadone, or something called "Ts and Blues" which was a mixture of two prescription drugs that was powdered, put into a liquid form, and injected. The mothers used this concoction during pregnancy, so of course, the babies were born addicted. Also, some of the physicians (residents mainly) seemed totally unable to see the parents' perspective, and the communication between parent and MD in these cases was extremely poor. Our conversation frequently focused on our observations. I guess we were beginning to find out that we valued the same things.

The Medici itself is still in Hyde Park, but in a different location now. They lost their lease in the original building and there was quite a lot of local uproar, petitions, etc., because it really is kind of a landmark. Eventually it moved down the block and across the street. Actually, I like the new location better, it has better lighting and is bigger, too.

Well, I didn't mean to go on and on about my personal history here! I don't know if it is the new year or what, but I'm starting to feel cautiously optimistic. Remember, I owe you a latte – so let me know when you want to collect! And I'm very anxious and curious to hear about your New Year celebration with Van – but only the amount of detail that you want to share, of course. (Just FYI, Pete will have Lauren for the next two weekends, since I had her over two holidays.) I need to email him next.

Take care.

Charlotte

To: Stone, Peter E
Date: Friday, January 2
From: Stone, Charlotte P
Subject: We're back

Hi Pete,

Just to let you know that Lauren and I made it back without any problems. Lauren is anxious to see you. Just let me know when you would like to pick her up.

Charlotte

To: Stone, Charlotte P
Date: Friday, January 2
From: Hansen, V
Subject: Re: Back home in Indiana

Hi Charlotte,

I'm glad to hear that you're back! My New Year's celebration was fantastic!! I would really like to tell you about it, too. I'm free on Sunday afternoon, if that works for you. We can meet at Starbucks if you like, and I'll collect on my bet!

I had to go back to work on the 2nd and that was kind of a bummer; we were really, really, busy. Everyone who was holding off on admissions over the holidays dumped on us...I think we had a total of six that were scheduled, plus some through the ER. I did two hours of overtime that day, and that is highly unusual, but there was no way around it.

Yes, it is a new year, and like you, I feel optimistic about it. Plus, even though I love Christmas, it is good to get the tree down. For one thing, it always makes my living room seem so much bigger. I enjoy the break of the holidays, but I also enjoy that "back to the routine" feeling.

Let me know what time might work for you re: coffee and conversation. I'm looking forward to plenty of both!

Veronica

To: Hansen, V
Date: Friday, January 2
From: Stone, Charlotte P
Subject: Re: Back home in Indiana

Hi Veronica,

You name the time and the particulars. I'll be free after 8AM tomorrow. Pete is going to pick up Lauren then. He will actually have her the next two weekends to "make up" for the time I had her over the holidays (if that makes sense). So tonight, Lauren and I will do her laundry, pretty much everything she needs to take with her is either dirty or brand new from Christmas and needs to be washed. My parents gave her some very cute pajamas that she wants to take with her.

The building is fairly quiet, but one family is here on the second floor. I like being able to hear others in the building, as long as the noises are typical.

So...let me know when and where, I'll be there.

Charlotte

To: Stone, Charlotte P
Date: Friday, January 2
From: Hansen, V
Subject: Meeting

Hi Charlotte – How about 2 PM on Sunday? I'm going to go to Mass at 11, and then I need to run a quick errand for Anna. We could meet at the Starbucks close to your apartment.

Veronica

To: Hansen, V
Date: Saturday, January 3
From: Stone, Charlotte P
Subject: Re: Meeting

OK – you're on for Sunday PM at 2.

When Pete came by this AM to pick up Lauren (and yes, if you are wondering, I did get up early to wash my hair and put on makeup.) He gave me a bud vase. This one was a silver/pewter color and the rose was pink. There was a kind of a cherub figure with it which, I suppose, is the New Year's baby. The little card said "Best of wishes for both of us in the New Year." Different, anyway. The vase is in our little entryway. It is very classy looking. There was baby's breath, too, and a large pink and silver ribbon.

Lauren was very glad to see Pete. She started describing her Christmas presents right away. Pete gave me a quick little "sideways" hug and was gone. I'll go over there about 7 PM tomorrow to pick her up, since the public schools reopen on Monday, and I want Lauren to get a good night's sleep.

See you tomorrow at Starbucks.

Charlotte

To: Hansen, V
Date: Monday, January 5
From: Stone, Charlotte P
Subject: Back to reality

Hi Veronica,

Hope your workday is going okay and that the post-holiday craziness is calming down. I've finished doing my four hours of work here in the office, the part I do to earn my stipend. After lunch, I'll start my other "work" of the unpaid variety; that is, studying for the qualifying exam.

I really enjoyed hearing about your New Year's Eve. Van deserves all kinds of points for thinking of taking you to a haunted bed and breakfast as part of the celebration. What a perfect place for two sleuths to ring in the New Year! I also enjoyed hearing about the "cold spots" in the house and the history of the "blue lady." The dinner sounded great, too.

Well, when I went to pick up Lauren, Pete's mom invited me in for sandwiches. Of course, I took her up on it, since I hadn't eaten since noon and I haven't replenished the refrigerator yet, I'll do that this afternoon. The supper was fun and fairly relaxed. They still have their tree up, because they like to leave it up until Twelfth Night.

Then they take it to the city park near their home for the annual bonfire.

While Pete's mom cleared the table and Pete's dad and Lauren went to gather up her things, Pete grabbed me by the elbow, marched me to the entry way and kissed me hard on the lips. Then he pointed to the mistletoe hanging from the light fixture, which I hadn't noticed before. That kiss left me feeling a little weak in the knees. I still don't get this kind of behavior from Pete. Does absence make the heart grow fonder? Is that what he is trying to figure out? I don't know – I only know that I liked being kissed under the mistletoe.

I think Lauren was ready to go back to school. She was up early and had dressed and combed her hair before I even got out of bed this morning!

Have a good one!

Charlotte

To: Stone, Charlotte P
Date: Monday, January 5
From: Hansen, V
Subject: Wild Day

Hi Charlotte,

Did you go "back to work" today? Our place was wild, not so much due to scheduled or ER admissions, but due to unscheduled nursing home admissions. In spite of the fact that most of the patient information is available from the facility itself, the process seems very, very slow. I don't know what we could do to improve it, but I'm sure we could figure out something if we could analyze the types of problems we always seem to have. Of course, the patients themselves are rarely violent; they are mostly depressed and sometimes almost catatonic. We can't get much information from them. We have a specialized gero-psych unit here. I've been up to their unit a few times, and I've always been impressed with what I see. Some of the patients end up coming to us for shock therapy, and it does seem to help many of them.

I'm having a hard time readjusting to reality after my magic New Year's celebration. Is this how it is for high school seniors after they've been to the prom? I wouldn't know, since my mom would never let me go. I think about things we (Van and I) did over the holiday, over and over…just like someone reliving their first kiss. I guess parts of us never grow up, no matter how old we get. Maybe that is a good thing!

Well, I'm going to do something that I don't often do – take a bubble bath, maybe with a glass of wine handy, before getting ready for bed! I'll take a novel with me, too. Robyn gave me an assortment of little bottles of scented bubble bath and bath oils for Christmas. I think I'll try one of those tonight.

Have a good evening.

Veronica

To: Hansen, V
Date: Tuesday, January 6
From: Stone, Charlotte P
Subject: Re: Wild Day

Hi Veronica,

Sorry that you had such a wild day yesterday. You always seem to handle the activity level so well. I think your workplace must really value you, because you always have this way of rising to the occasion. That was true at St. J's, too, even if we had to put a patient in restraints. You were always efficient and organized about whatever needed to be done.

My day was a direct contrast to yours, in many ways. I took Lauren to school, then I came back to the apartment and showered before going in to work. It was quiet there, about a third of the staff were still out for the holidays. The statisticians were in for a moment, and I mentioned my finding about the older women briefly. Their response was not to worry, it was way too early. I should wait until I have at least 50 more people in each of the four categories I'm looking at before making any conclusions. That will take at least another month, maybe more. Actually, I don't think that the statisticians were ready to think that hard so soon after the holidays. I'll also mention my findings to Pete and Dr. Fleming. Anyhow, I got my cubicle reorganized and caught up on the tasks I've been hired to do as a research assistant for her project. It felt kind of good to do that. Another strange email in my university inbox...I guess I'm getting used to them. It merely said "Try as hard as you want, you will never succeed. You don't have a clue about science. Your genetic makeup is lacking." Whatever!

When I got home last night, Pete called. He wants to take me out for my birthday, and his parents will watch Lauren. After Lauren and I ate dinner, (which was late due to Pete's phone call; we chatted quite a bit), I spent time helping her with her homework. Then it was time for bed, for both of us. I was exhausted for some reason. I feel great today after nine hours of sleep.

Anyhow, I've put in my four hours on Dr. Fleming's project, so now I'm headed over to the library to study for the qualifying exam. Maybe I'll be able to take it at the end of the month after all. I'll see how it goes. I won't see Dr. Fleming until next week, probably, so I have almost a week to see how well I can concentrate.

Hope today is less wild at your workplace. Take care.

Charlotte

PS – Did I tell you that the SomaRx "Christmas Party" has been scheduled for January 15th? That should be interesting.

To: Stone, Charlotte P
Date: Tuesday, January 6
From: Hansen, V
Subject: Re: Wild Day

Hi Charlotte,

Well, today was much calmer except for one really weird event. A young woman (who had consented to having electroconvulsive therapy, of course) starting screaming bloody murder just as the anesthesiologist was starting the premedication. She had long curly red hair and a very pale complexion. For some reason, the first thing I thought of was the movie "Carrie." However, the screaming only lasted a minute and then she was calm as the medication took effect. It was an unnerving experience. Several people made strange jokes about calling a priest and needing some holy water. The patient was fine after she regained consciousness. I've never seen anything like it. But, after that was over the rest of the day went smoothly.

Right before I went home, I started an admission and the social worker took over for me when it was time for me to leave. I called from home because I forgot to ask what time the earliest ECT was scheduled for tomorrow before I left. Evidently, the person being admitted went all the way through the admission process, then decided that they didn't want to be hospitalized after all. I hate it when that happens!! At least I didn't stay overtime for that!

OK, don't be mad at me – but exactly what day is your birthday? I know it is in the first half of January, but I forget the exact date. Hopefully, you and Pete will have a good time when the day rolls around.

I hope your study time was productive today. Have a good evening.

Veronica

To: Stone, Charlotte P
Date: Wednesday, January 7
From: Oberon
Subject: Soon

Hello, my sweet. A new year, time for a new love. I will claim you soon.

Oberon

To: Hansen, V
Date: Wednesday, January 7
From: Stone, Charlotte P
Subject: My birthday

Hi Veronica,

I'm not mad! I know your birthday is sometime in mid-October, but I'm not sure of the exact date either. Mine is January 11, this Sunday. Pete has told me to keep the afternoon and evening open, so I'm doing that.

My birthday is generally a cold, cold day. Plus it is too close to the holidays, so most people are tired of celebrations and presents. But, not much I can do about it: I guess I'm stuck with it for the rest of my life!! Maybe I'll celebrate it in the southern hemisphere sometime, at least it will be warm. (By the way, did I tell you that Alejandro was born in Argentina? I thought of that, because he has a January birthday, too. When he was little, his birthday was in the summer, until his family moved to this country.) Also, by the way – are you going to go to him and get your hair cut? You really won't regret it!!

I'm enjoying the quietness on campus for this week. Lauren is glad for the structure of being back in school. She's also enjoyed wearing the new clothes that she got for Christmas. I am able to concentrate. I'm studying for the qualifying exam on a schedule, 3 to 4 hours every afternoon, or split between afternoon and evening. I need to tell Dr. Fleming next week whether I will take the exam at the end of the month or wait until March.

Pete has Lauren again this weekend. I may treat myself to a manicure or something with some of my Christmas money. If I were braver, maybe I'd get a tattoo. However, I can't help but wonder what it would look like when I'm 70. In the future, will nursing home patients be known to their caregivers by their tattoos? I wonder. I don't think a wrinkled tattoo would look very attractive.

Oh by the way, I got another email from "Oberon." These messages don't even phase me anymore. In fact, I think they're kind of boring.

Have a good day!

Charlotte

To: Stone, Charlotte P
Date: Thursday, January 8
From: Hansen, V
Subject: Wrinkled Tattoos!

Hi Charlotte,

Wrinkled tattoos! No, I don't think they would look very attractive, either. I can't say I've seen too many on older women. Older guys, yes...ones who have been in the service...or in prison. The prison ones are the home-made, ball-point pen variety, though. Yes, I think I'll pass on the tattoos.

Well, my birthday is the 18th of October. Usually a pretty time of year, although sometimes my birthday is cold and rainy. When I was little, my dad took me driving on my birthday through Brown County. Usually, we'd start out at Schultz's for breakfast. I would usually get some kind of bagel and top it off with a potato pancake. Then we'd head south and stop at one of the great restaurants in Nashville for a "down-home" lunch with plenty of fried biscuits and apple butter (no one was counting carbohydrates back then.) Sometimes, my Dad would even let me skip school for the day. My mother never wanted to come, so it was just the two of us. We had some real quality father-daughter time.

Well, I need to go. I'm on my break at work, and decided to come up to the library to look up something. But now I need to get back as I have an admission coming in. So far, it has been quiet, since we don't do ECT on Thursdays. Hopefully, it is not the calm before the storm!

Have a good day.

Veronica

PS Do you have the phone number for Alejandro's salon?

To: Hansen, V
Date: Thursday, January 8
From: Stone, Charlotte P
Subject: Re: Wrinkled Tattoos!

Hi Veronica,

I don't have the number for the salon on me, but it is listed in both the white and yellow pages and online. (Village Trail Salon). Alejandro also has a Facebook page. I like the fact that you can get in within a day or two. That way, I just wait until I have a couple of bad hair days in a row – then I know it is time to pay Alejandro a visit. Besides giving great haircuts, he is a lot of fun to talk to. He is a very creative person. In fact, sometimes I tell myself that I need a "dose of Alejandro" whether or not I need a haircut. He is such a good listener, which amazes me. And I think in his line of work, he has probably heard it all!

OK, now it is my turn to ask. Do you know where I can get a good manicure (they don't have anyone who does that at Village Trail.) I am going to seriously consider getting one either tomorrow or Saturday, if I can.

By the time you read this, your workday should be over. Hopefully it ended without any major disasters. Take care.

Charlotte

To: Stone, Charlotte P
Date: Friday, January 9
From: Hansen, V
Subject: Manicure

Charlotte,

You can get a good manicure at a place in the strip mall on Georgetown Road. It is just a few doors down from the grocery. I forget the name. They are somewhat busy on weekends, but even if you walk in, they will be able to take you in 30 to 40 minutes. Just take a book along to read, or run an errand if you have to wait.

Yes, my workday did end without any major disasters. That was nice for a change! A couple of people did leave early (without permission, I might add), but for once it didn't matter because all of the work was done for the week. Most of the time, when people pull that stunt, there is still work to do. They never get any consequences for that either, at least that I am aware of. To me, that behavior is amazingly rude and unprofessional. It's equally amazing to me that no one loses their job over it. Maybe I'm just hopelessly old-fashioned.

I'm going to take Robyn to the bookstore tomorrow, then we'll go for lunch to McDonald's. The restaurant was her choice. So, we'll have a little grandmother-granddaughter time. We're going to the bookstore because she wants to buy some Nancy Drew books. She has some Christmas money to spend. On Thanksgiving, she found some of my old Nancy Drew books and took one home. She's since come back for another one. (I think she's hooked!) So now, she wants to buy some of the newer ones for herself :-D!

Have a good day tomorrow. Pamper yourself!

Veronica

To: Hansen, V
Date: Saturday, January 10
From: Stone, Charlotte P
Subject: New Nails

Hi Veronica,

Good old Nancy Drew! I definitely was hooked from second grade through junior high on those books. I still remember being so scared by "The Hidden Staircase" that I couldn't sleep! I still think I'm a frustrated detective, but I try to apply my sleuthing to research now. Once I made that comment to another member of the team and she looked at me like I had grown two heads. I've learned to keep those thoughts to myself!

Well, I went to the place that you suggested for a manicure, and it was really enjoyable. The girl that did my nails was friendly and chatty. She is from Vietnam, and she speaks English very well. She says she learned some English before leaving Vietnam, but once she got here (in the States) she realized her English was not very good. So every time she had enough money, she went to the movies. She said that improved her English very quickly as far as the spoken language goes. To improve her knowledge of the written language, she rents movies and watches them with subtitles. Sound like a great idea!

I would love to be able to buy something new for my "date" with Pete, but I really can't justify spending any extra money on something like that right now. But I happened to run into my former boss at the campus bookstore the other day. She's not enrolling in any classes, but she was looking around for references to keep at work. She has clothes out the wazoo. I was telling her about my "date"...and she said she had a dress she would give me (and I didn't even mention my poor wardrobe situation!) She must have me pegged as a bad dresser. Anyhow, she is going to come over here this PM with three dresses and she says I can have my pick. She says, since her divorce, she doesn't need all of the dress-up clothes. She'll give one to me because she knows that I will have to shorten it and she says that is okay, I can just have it! I can't turn down a deal like that!

Lauren is at Pete's right now, so it is quiet here. I'm going to study for qualifying exams for a while...after I make a pot of coffee! Definitely need that brain stimulation before tackling these huge textbooks and reading about statistics!

Have a good Saturday,

Charlotte

To: Stone, Charlotte P
Date: Sunday, January 11
From: Hansen, V
Subject: HAPPY BIRTHDAY!

Hi Charlotte,

Hope your day is starting off on a happy note. It just now hit me that Lauren wouldn't be there in the AM to wish you a happy day. But I know that you will see her tonight.

I'm glad that you liked the manicure salon. I don't go there often, but once in a while I treat myself for a special occasion. Actually, I got both a manicure and a pedicure for my special New Year's Eve celebration with Van. But I took all of the polish off before heading back to work. I knew someone who actually died of a staph infection that came from a hangnail. She always had those plastic-type nails. So, I always have "bare nails" when I am at work. I think it is safer for me and the patients, too.

Did you find a dress that you liked from your boss's "closet sale?" Did you shorten it yourself? Are you good at that kind of thing (dress alterations)?

I will have a gift for you the next time that I see you. It is just something small, but something I enjoy a lot so I thought that you might like it, too. Maybe we can meet for coffee in a week or two.

Enjoy your day,

Veronica

To: Hansen, V
Date: Sunday, January 11
From: Stone, Charlotte P
Subject: Thanks!

Hi Veronica,

Thank you for the birthday greeting. You really don't need to get me any gift, but I'll look forward to meeting you for coffee before too long. That's always fun! It adds balance to my life. I can only study and work for so long.

I saw Lauren at church. She went to Sunday School, Pete dropped her off and picked her up. It is only a few blocks from his parents' place. People at church have started to notice that I am attending alone. But no one has come out and asked me where Pete is, and I just don't feel like volunteering the information. Lauren gave me a big hug, and she had made me a card that was very, very cute. She said she would give me a present when she came home tonight.

Well, as far as the "closet sale," Tina (my former boss) brought over three dresses as she promised. The one I ended up choosing was different from anything I'd ever worn before. In fact, until I tried it on, I wouldn't have thought that I would like it. For one thing, the color is a little different – it is a pewter gray satin-like fabric, and it is sleeveless with spaghetti straps. It also has a little stole that goes with it. The bodice is beaded, and it has a slim skirt with a back slit. And even though I'm at least three inches shorter than Tina, I don't need to shorten it after all, because the length looks okay and there are no sleeves to worry about. (But yes, I can do alterations for myself.) I have a set of (fake) Tahitian pearls that I'll wear with it, and Tina even had some pewter-colored long gloves that she also gave me. My hair is still long enough (barely) to put up, and I went to Kohl's and got a pewter hair ornament to hold it in place. So, I'm set! Pete still hasn't told me where we're going, but he did say that it will be someplace very nice. I'm looking forward to it.

So, for right now, I'm treating myself to sitting in the arm chair in my sweats, reading a mystery and drinking some of my favorite coffee. I'll start getting ready in about an hour and I'll update you after my big evening!

Have a relaxing Sunday afternoon.

Charlotte

To: Hansen, V
Date: Monday, January 12
From: Stone, Charlotte P
Subject: Oh my...!

Hi Veronica,

Where do I start? I had an unusual, but very enjoyable birthday! Pete picked me up at 4:30 and told me that we needed to work up an appetite. At first, I wondered if that was supposed to be a suggestive statement and I must have looked puzzled. But he just said – "Where's your coat?" When we got down downstairs, there was a horse and carriage waiting. We got in and took off for a ride around the downtown area. (There are some advantages to living close to campus!) The afternoon was gray with a few flakes of snow, but it wasn't too cold, and Pete had a bottle of wine and two glasses in the carriage. By the time we got back to the apartment, about an hour later, the lights were coming on. It was a very, very pretty picture, with the snow flurries and everything. After the carriage took off, we got into Pete's car and we took off for the Canterbury. I'd been there for tea long ago, but never for a meal. The dining room is small and intimate, with lots of dark wood and tables in different nooks and crannies. We had our own nook. Pete sat next to me and had his hand on my leg until the appetizer arrived. I guess the food was supposed to be like higher-class pub food, or something on that order. It was good, and different. Pete kissed me a couple of times... we had enough privacy for that. Also, there were other diners, but it wasn't crowded. Mostly we talked about our past. I brought up my recent visit to the Medici, and how it made me think about our early history as a couple.

From this romantic setting we drove to his parents' house. We picked up Lauren. When we got back to the apartment, I took off my coat, of course, and Lauren said, "Ooh, you look pretty, Mommie!" Pete winked at her. Lauren did seem tired. I helped her get ready for bed and she fell asleep almost as soon as her head hit her pillow. Then Pete went down to his car. He came back with two packages... very nicely wrapped, I might add. One was small, one was much larger.

In the first was a pair of earrings. They were small hoops, with tiny diamonds outlining the hoop. (Remember the movie *Crossing Delancey*? I was being wooed!)

The second box was the size of a shirt box. I opened it, then pushed aside the tissue paper. I recognized the contents. It was a pair of old pajamas – Pete's pajamas! He kissed my neck and said "Can I spend the night?"

The scene fades at this point. . .

Back to reality in the morning. Lauren was very excited to see Pete there. (He meant to leave before she got up, but it didn't work out that way.) Lauren, of course, hoped that Daddy was back for good, but he handled that extremely well. He gave me a kiss on the cheek and said that he would be emailing me later. He also took Lauren to school.

Now, I'm the one with the senior-prom syndrome. About my husband of twelve-plus years. Amazing! Studying was difficult today.

Hope your day went well!

Charlotte

To: Stone, Charlotte P
Date: Monday, January 12
From: Stone, Peter E
Subject: Postscript

Hi Charlotte,

I hope you enjoyed your birthday. I did. In answer to your question about my vision for the future...yes, I do see us getting back together. I just don't know when. This arrangement may not be conventional, but you have to admit, we have stopped fighting and we are appreciating each other more. When I look at these words on the screen, they seem kind of harsh and don't exactly express what I mean. Maybe what I'm trying to say is that I am making progress and I think we are, too, as a couple.

I do miss you and love you.

Pete

To: Stone, Charlotte P
Date: Monday, January 12
From: Hansen, V
Subject: Re: Oh, my...!

Hello Charlotte,

Well, your subject line pretty much sums it up! You have to give Pete credit. It seems like he planned a birthday that you would really enjoy, and that gave you the opportunity to feel very special. He is creative, too. I like the pajamas-wrapped-in-a-box idea. Your birthday could be the beginning of progress in your relationship.

My Sunday was exciting, but not in the way yours was. Both of my kids are experiencing relationship problems. Nothing that they can't handle, but as a mom, I still worry about my kids. For some reason, this weekend I worried more than I usually do. Van is very busy on a case, so I did not see him. Maybe that is why I'm worried. I tried to read, study, and clean up my condo, but nothing really seemed to help. Today, I was back to the work routine, and I feel better. Plus, Van is going to meet me in Pendleton for dinner. He is going to give me some detective work to do for him, so it will be a "working dinner." But it will be good to see him.

Well, my lunch is over. I need to get back to the unit.

Veronica

To: Stone, Charlotte P
Date: Tuesday, January 13
From: Oberon
Subject: My Review

Titania,

You looked beautiful in your silver dress. I cannot wait to possess you. I await the time that you are in my arms.

Oberon

To: Hansen, V
Date: Tuesday, January 13
From: Stone, Charlotte P
Subject: Developments

Hi Veronica,

Once again, I'm battling the urge to hyperventilate. Another message from "Oberon" in my personal email account. And it refers to my "silver dress" which I assume is the one I wore on my birthday. I'm majorly creeped out. I reported it to my ISP.

In addition to that, things never stop happening, I guess. First of all, I told Dr. Fleming that I would be able to take the qualifying exam at the end of the month. I've had some productive study time over the holidays and the first part of January. And the sooner that I get the qualifying exam over with, the sooner I will be able to concentrate on my dissertation. I should get another set of data from the biostatistics people any day now.

Secondly, I got a call from Max! He said he was cashing in his rain check for coffee. As he put it, it is now "after the holidays," which it is, so I said I would meet him near campus on Thursday afternoon for an hour. It will be kind of a late lunch break. We'll probably meet at Starbucks. I'm going to keep it superficial and friendly. He had better not have his hopes up about a big romance. He probably doesn't, but I feel somewhat on guard.

Then, the next day is the SomaRx "post-holiday" party. I decided to go. I will just play it by ear. It is actually in the afternoon, too. I will need to leave early anyway to get Lauren from school, so if it gets too painful, I'll leave even earlier! But I don't think that any disasters will happen. After all, things are going well between Pete and me.

Hope your evening with Van went well!!

Charlotte

To: Stone, Charlotte P
Date: Wednesday, January 14
From: Hansen, V
Subject: WOW!

Charlotte,

I love my hair and I think Alejandro is terrific!! I love to listen and he has interesting things to tell. My hair just looks and feels fantastic. We both agree that today was just the first step. I want to let it grow out a little more, have it in better condition and change the color to a softer blond, like a wheat blond. I can't believe the difference in how I feel! I went in feeling tired and frumpy and came out full of energy with hair that looks great, feels great, and moves great. I need to work on my makeup a little, change my wardrobe a little, and lose some weight. I will be quite polished in the near future! I think Van will be impressed. I have my next appointment with Alejandro in 6 weeks. He says he thinks you are cool and very smart and he always takes something with him from your conversations. He talked about his hiking, camping, and caving. He does his own car and home repairs and even sews! He is a kind of Renaissance man!

Today was hectic at work. And it started getting worse as the day went on. By the time to leave, I just practically ran out the door. I didn't want to be late for my appointment and it's easy for the momentum to pull you in and half an hour later you are still trying to pull yourself loose. Liz is working harder than she was. I know she doesn't want to lose her job and I think my boss made it plain that she needed to straighten up and fly right.

I think you are pretty safe going for a one-hour "lunch" with Max. You have a definite ending point, so not too much can happen. Plus you will both have to go back to work. Just be honest with him; you are not really a "single woman." At least it doesn't seem like you are viewing yourself as single to me.

Thanks again for the hair stylist referral. I can't believe the difference when I look in the mirror!

Take care – Veronica

To: Stone, Charlotte P
Date: Wednesday, January 14
From: Hansen, V
Subject: Your concern

Charlotte – Sorry, I didn't address your fears about the strange email. You must have thought that I was very insensitive. I agree that this latest email sounds like it is more personal. Reporting this one sounds like a good idea. Maybe even to the police, as well as your ISP. I still wouldn't lose sleep over it, though. Most people who do this type of thing are basically cowards.

Veronica

To: Hansen, V
Date: Wednesday, January 14
From: Stone, Charlotte P
Subject: You're right

Hi Veronica,

Yes, you are right: I don't view myself as a single woman. And you are also right: not much can happen in an hour. I'm pretty safe going for this coffee meeting with Max, and I do need to eat lunch. I'll go to the library and study for quals afterwards.

This Friday party at SomaRx is going to be interesting. It is hard to get excited about a party in the middle of the day after the holidays are over. I wonder why they are even bothering to go through with it. Maybe the woman who is back from maternity leave is feeling guilty or "incomplete" because she hasn't carried this out yet. We'll see. It sounds like a pretty tame event to me.

I think that I should write to Pete. I haven't answered his email from Monday yet. Next week is our first research meeting together since the holidays.

Yes, I did decide that I should not delete the "Oberon" email. If it continues, I'll have evidence of the pattern. I was able to find the first one in my "deleted" folder, so I started a separate folder and put both the new one and the old one into it. I'm hoping that I don't need to add any more. I'm starting to have a little problem with sleeping. I hope that doesn't continue.

Are you doing any detective assignments for Van now? Have a good day at work.

Charlotte

To: Stone, Peter E
Date: Wednesday, January 14
From: Stone, Charlotte P
Subject: Re: Postscript

Hello Pete,

Yes, I did have a wonderful time on my birthday. I am glad to know that you did, too. Yes, this arrangement is unconventional, and yes, I don't miss the fighting. But I do miss you. I think I would put up with the fighting to have you here all of the time. I am glad that you see us making progress and especially that you see us getting together again in the future.

Are you going to the party on Friday?

Love,

Charlotte

To: Stone, Charlotte P
Date: Thursday, January 15
From: Stone, Peter E
Subject: Re: Postscript

Yes, I plan on being there.

Pete

To: Hansen, V
Date: Thursday, January 15
From: Stone, Charlotte P
Subject: Lunch Date

Hi Veronica,

Well, I had my lunch with Max. It went okay. As it turned out, I felt pretty relaxed when one o'clock rolled around. I felt a little nervous about it yesterday. Starbucks was still pretty noisy and busy at 1:00, so I didn't feel pressured to be the great conversationalist or anything like that. But we had enough to talk about and it was kind of fun.

Mostly, we talked about research. Max is involved in some pediatric research concerning colic. Almost everyone else on the project is female. There is one female physician and three nurses. One is a doctorally prepared nurse and the other two have their master's – one is a pediatric nurse practitioner and the other is a clinical nurse specialist. And of course, they have a statistician. It sounds like an interesting project. I think Max is having a relatively tough time though, being the only male on the team. It sounds like there are some communication issues and maybe a few "cat fights" – although he didn't really say that directly. Mostly I just listened.

At one point he said, "You know, I recently separated, too." And I said, "I'm not really separated." And he said, "Hmmmm, you're not living together, right? Do you have plans to reunite? Are you in counseling?" Then he just smiled. So, I guess he was saying that I am separated, and maybe that I'm even in denial (?) Then the conversation went back to safer topics.

As we got ready to leave, he said he had a family wedding to go to at the end of the month. He asked me to go with him. He said there would be no "pressure," whatever that means, but it would be easier on him if he had a date. He said I could just go to the reception with him for a couple of hours. It is here, in town, at "the Mansion" on the St. Catherine College campus. I told him I would think about it. So – that is how it ended. Except for the comments about "separation," it was fairly painless.

How was your day? Hopefully it went well.

Charlotte

To: Stone, Charlotte P
Date: Thursday, January 15
From: Hansen, V
Subject: Re: Lunch Date

Hi Charlotte,

Well, I'm going to go into my protective, "mother hen" mode. Maybe I'm just in a weird mood, but all kinds of red flags are popping up in my head. First of all, the "no pressure" line. In my experience, that always means that there is going to be some kind of pressure. Secondly, the "I'm separated, too" line. Maybe he views you as a prime target for mutual consolation. Thirdly, the wedding angle. A lot of guys look at unattached women who are attending weddings as easy targets. So, there you have it, my "big three" areas of concern!

But, that said, it doesn't mean that I'm telling you not to go. If you want to, go ahead and take the opportunity to get out and have some fun. Just have your guard up. On the plus side, it was somewhat sensitive of Max to give you "permission" not to attend the wedding itself, given your situation. He does get a point or two for that. Also, you are both involved with research, so that gives you something safe (and relatively dry, in my opinion :-D!) to talk about. Actually, I think that the colic project sounds interesting. And Max must have some people skills if he is in pediatrics and can get along with that many women on a project.

My workplace is the most dysfunctional place in the world, I can tell you that! It is one of those standing psych jokes that you can't always tell the staff from the patients, and that is absolutely true. One of the nurses is planning on having a minor outpatient surgery and trying to get six or more weeks off for that. I'm glad I don't really have to get into those kind of issues. I just stick to my work, get it done as efficiently as possible, and go home and concentrate on the rest of my life. Things are going pretty well. I saw all of the grandkids last weekend and both kids seem to have their individual minor crises settled, at least for now. Life is pretty good. I'm not going to take on any more problems than I have to.

Well, let me know how the SomaRx "alternative-Christmas" party goes! It should be interesting at any rate!

Take care – Veronica

To: Hansen, V
Date: Friday, January 16
From: Stone, Charlotte P
Subject: Post Party

Veronica:

I am so angry that I can hardly see straight. The funny thing is, I really don't have a right to be angry, I guess. What happened at the party was relatively minor – on the surface. But put it this way – I did not have a good time!

First of all, I guess I didn't know exactly what to expect, but I did expect to have some fun. This would be the first time that Pete and I had been together since my birthday celebration last weekend. I totally expected to have some kind of positive contact with him.

It was different having this get-together in the middle of the afternoon during a non-holiday time of the year. The room was barely decorated with some sloppy-looking snowflakes. The refreshments looked like holiday leftovers. (Usually, the party is pretty impressive in the decoration and food departments.) Because I had to leave early to get Lauren, I went early. I was one of the first ones there. One of the statisticians, who also has children, was there, too. We struck up a conversation. I really didn't know her well before this, but we seem to have a lot in common.

Then people started to arrive in greater numbers. I said hello to a couple of the people who work on the project with Dr. Fleming. The room started to get somewhat crowded. About a half an hour prior to the time that I had to leave, Pete arrived with some other pharmacists. Among them was Trish, the new Purdue graduate who was an intern two summers ago. She was hired on in August. Well, she and Pete were apparently engrossed in some very earnest conversation. They hardly stopped talking to each other, and the other pharmacists in the group brought them food and drinks. I had to leave, so I walked by and said Hello, and Pete said that a group from their office was going out together after the party and he invited me. But, he also had to have known that I would turn down the invitation because I had to get Lauren. So, I left, feeling left out and ignored. Maybe my expectations were too high, but still ...I'm angry. You know that old saying "Why buy a cow when milk is so cheap?" Well, maybe that saying applies to me, somewhat. And not divorcing can work to Pete's advantage, too, since he has an excuse to not commit to anyone else. So he can get milk from two cows. Sorry, I'm not making too much sense here, and my grammar is terrible, I know – but maybe Max was right about the separated status and maybe I've been in denial, especially the past week.

So, I called Max and told him to count on me for the wedding, including the ceremony!

Charlotte

To: Stone, Charlotte P
Date: Friday, January 16
From: Hansen, V
Subject: Re: Post Party

Hi Charlotte,

Well, I wouldn't be too upset about the party thing. After all, you had to leave early. Pete did make an effort to include you. But, I do understand your feelings as well. And it won't hurt to go to the wedding with Max, if that is what you want to do. When is it exactly? And remind me, what did you decide about the qualifying exam? Are you going to take it at the end of the month?

Van and I are going out to dinner tonight in Morristown. He gets together about once a year, usually after the holidays, with a family that he met several years ago on a case. Some guy tried to burn up the entire family by setting the house on fire in the early AM hours before dawn. The family that we'll be eating dinner with pulled several family members out of the burning house. Only one person died, which is sad, but it could have been four people. Van was involved with the case as it went to trial. That's how he met this family, and he stays in touch with them. (The perpetrator is now behind bars, where he should be!)

Work is very interesting. Quite a few people seem to get angry if they actually have to do work! You seem to see that attitude everywhere, especially in retail. Clerks can look really angry if you ask them for any help whatsoever. An exception occurred last weekend when I took Allen and his kids out to eat. The host was extremely helpful and friendly, without overdoing it, from the minute we entered the door until the time we left with all of our "doggie bags." I feel like I should officially commend him to somebody; maybe I'll look into it. I'm all for giving credit where credit is due.

What are you doing this weekend?

Veronica

To: Hansen, V
Date: Saturday, January 17
From: Stone, Charlotte P
Subject: Answers

Hi Veronica,

Well, to answer the last question you asked: STUDYING!!! That is what I am going to do this weekend, mainly. I will study for the qualifying exam and work on the data that will become the basis for my dissertation. I picked up some more data before the party started on Thursday. I have yet to add it to the rest and examine the patterns in it. I'm hoping the symptoms in the older women have moderated with more people in the sample. If they haven't, well, I won't be exactly sure how to proceed. I guess I'll ask Dr. Fleming about how to handle things if that becomes necessary. But I can't ignore the data just because I'm afraid of what I might find there. We'll see. I plan to study first, until I can no longer stand it; then I'll look at and play around with the new data if I have time.

In answer to your other question, the wedding is the last weekend of the month. It's an evening event. The ceremony probably won't be too long. It is going to be held at the college chapel and then the bridal party will just walk a block or two on the St. Catherine campus to the mansion where the reception will be. The mansion looks beautiful on the outside. It is on a hilltop. I imagine before the interstate cut through the area, you could probably see the river from the windows. I guess it was owned by a wealthy auto manufacturer originally. When he died, he left it to the religious order, and the college started out in that building.

I guess I'll wear the pewter outfit that I wore on my birthday. It should be okay for an evening wedding. I offered to return it to Tina, but she said she didn't want it, wearing it brought back too many painful memories. Hmph! Maybe it is destined to become the "bad memory dress." Hopefully, I can put an end to the curse.

Come to think of it, I'm not even sure who is getting married, other than a family member of Max's. I think I will call him right now and get some of the particulars about the wedding. At least this is one wedding that I won't have to buy a gift for!

Charlotte

To: Stone, Charlotte P
Date: Sunday, January 18
From: Hansen, V
Subject: Mother Hen

Hi Charlotte,

OK, I have to go back into the mother hen mode for just a moment – be careful. Don't go after Max just because you happen to be disappointed in Pete at the moment. The whole experience could cascade into something awful. If you need to escape, or concentrate on something else, try channeling that energy into studying, if you can.

All right, I'm done giving advice. Do you have Lauren this weekend or next? I've lost track, for some reason. How is she doing lately? Any more concern from her re: Daddy coming back home?

Van and I went on an excursion to the east side of the state related to a case yesterday. It is almost a cold case, really, and has a medical spin. A physician lost his license (temporarily) related to an alleged mercy killing. The details at the time were hazy at best, and the

MD's record other than this one incident is as clean as a whistle, which is kind of unusual when you work in the ER. In that type of environment, someone will accuse you of something sooner or later. But this guy had 15 years of absolutely nothing in the way of accusations. Then, this one incident resulted in the loss of privileges for a year. He was reinstated, and has had a clean record ever since. However, someone seems to think that not everything was revealed originally (we're talking ten years ago). This "someone" is Van's client, and I don't even know who it is, and I don't want to know! But this "someone" seems to think that not all of the details of the mercy killing were revealed and that led to the MD getting off too easily, in the client's opinion. We went to interview a couple of witnesses, RNs who were working the shift in question in the ER. One RN is female; the other is male. We interviewed them individually. They both told the same story. And yes, it does appear that certain details were not brought to light, which really would change my take of the situation if I were in charge of deciding what charges should be filed against this MD. It was an interesting afternoon. Also, it was a pretty drive over there, the sun was shining. After interviewing the two witnesses, we went to dinner in a little family owned bar/restaurant that Van goes to when he is in that neck of the woods. The food was very tasty, and the matriarch of the family still ruled the kitchen. She looked like she was about 85 years old. More power to her!

Well, I've gone on and on about this situation. Time to get back to work...my house is a wreck. Have a good Sunday! I hope your studying is going well.

Veronica

To: Hansen, V
Date: Sunday, January 18
From: Stone, Charlotte P
Subject: Re: Mother Hen

Hi Veronica,

Well, it is okay for you to give me advice now and then! I do appreciate it. And yes, you are right...I can't use my anger at Pete as a reason to throw myself at Max. I'll be rational!

I did call Max last night, and we chatted for about 15 minutes. It is his cousin that is getting married for the second time. The family thinks it is really inappropriate for her to have a second "big" wedding. He filled me in on some other family dynamics. He sounded pleased when I told him that I would attend the ceremony. When I hung up, the phone rang again within 5 minutes. It was Pete. He chatted about this and that. I asked him if he could take Lauren the evening of the wedding. I just told him that I had a wedding that I wanted to attend. He asked "Anyone I know?" and I said "No." He agreed without hesitation. So, I've got the childcare covered.

I will think of the reception as an earned evening out after studying for quals. I'll take the exam on the 30th, and will be ready to celebrate the minute I'm done.

As I've said before, your life is never dull. Interviewing witnesses to a mercy killing is not something I do in my life! However, I did get a preliminary look at the new data. And yes – the same trends are continuing. Women older than 45 do not appear to be doing well on this new drug. So, now what do I do? I think I will tell Pete first. I haven't mentioned it to him yet. I want to run some more stats and develop the entire picture first, so I have all of my "ducks in a row" before showing him what I have found. I will also probably tell Dr. Fleming because she is my mentor, and because she also does research with this group. I'm hoping either she or Pete will take care of whatever you are supposed to do in situations like this. That is all that I know to do. I almost wish that I hadn't found it. It complicates things. But, like I said – I need to run some more figures before I do anything else.

Well, another Sunday night – the weeks seem to go by so quickly. Take care.

Charlotte

To: Stone, Charlotte P
Date: Monday, January 19
From: Strong, James Y
Subject: Re: Query: Central College Days??

Hi! I was watching the History Channel and they were featuring an Army sergeant during WWI named Proesser. He received a citation for bravery. Any relation?

All the best

Jim

James Y Strong, PhD
Dean, School of Science
South Central State

To: Strong, James Y
Date: Monday, January 19
From: Stone, Charlotte P
Subject: Re: Query: Central College Days??

Interesting! Not that I know of. But, the west coast side of my family doesn't communicate with the Midwesterners much. There's been quite a turnover due to divorce, I'm not even sure of all of their names. CS

To: Stone, Charlotte P
Date: Monday, January 19
From: Strong, James Y
Subject: Re: Query: Central College Days??

Actually, this guy's grandson lives in Chicago. He may be from the Midwestern side of your family!

All the best

Jim

James Y Strong, PhD
Dean, School of Science
South Central State

To: Hansen, V
Date: Monday, January 19
From: Stone, Charlotte P
Subject: Guess What?

Hi Veronica,

Guess what – I got another email from the dean at South Central State. Just a short message, kind of like casual conversation. I don't know why he does this, but I have to admit – I think that it is kind of fun.

Today, there are no classes due to Martin Luther King Day, which makes it an excellent day to study. I took Lauren over to a friend's house this morning. They are going to play there until about 2PM. Then I'll go pick her up and bring both of them back to our apartment for a while. I should still be able to study. Alexis's dad will pick her up between 5:30 and 6.

I feel pretty good about things. I am looking forward to the wedding with Max, don't ask me why. I like Max well enough, I guess, but I don't have any romantic thoughts about him. I think it is just the idea of getting dressed up and having fun and having "no pressure," although, I will remember your advice. I am also looking forward to having the qualifying exam over!!

While Lauren and Alexis are playing, I'm going to look through the data again. I'll print off some of the figures. Then I'll take it with me to the meeting on Thursday. Even though the statisticians are looking at the data in the early stages, I guess they don't run any inferential statistics, just basically descriptive stuff. I know that they are not doing what I am doing, splitting the males and females into two groups by age, so I have four groups total: Older men, younger men, older women, and younger women. The older women are markedly different. They are not showing the therapeutic effect of the drug and they are having significantly more side effects from it. I'm surprised that more aren't dropping out of the study. But, it is still early. However, I'm sure that the older women are a large part of the potential market for this drug. The fact that they are not getting any benefit from it (apparently) and having more side effects doesn't bode well for future drug sales.

Well, coffee break is over, I need to get back to work!

Charlotte

To: Stone, Charlotte P
Date: Monday, January 19
From: Hansen, V
Subject: Re: Guess What?

Hi Charlotte,

Well, it is kind of interesting that the professor, or whoever he is, is emailing you again. It sounds like a source of safe excitement for you, anyway.

I'll be curious to hear more about what these data are showing you. I'm not really too interested in statistics, but if that many people aren't doing well on the new drug...well...that is very interesting. And because I do work in psych, I am interested in depression, and treatments for it. People certainly don't need to be throwing their money away on drugs that don't work.

Also, you should have fun at the wedding when it rolls around. You have worked hard, you've been through all kinds of stress in the last few months...so, after you take the exam, you are entitled to a little fun. I went to a reception at that mansion on the St. Catherine campus about ten years ago. It was lovely.

How neat that Lauren has a little playmate that she can spend that much time with and enjoy. that will help you out with your studying as well.

Van is going out of town for a week to do some kind of forensics update training. It is in Kansas, of all places. He will leave next Monday and be back on Friday. I'll miss him, but the week will go by fast. I'll be interested in all he learns, also. It will almost be like going myself, because I will review all of the learning materials with him afterwards.

Happy studying!

Veronica

To: Hansen, V
Date: Tuesday, January 20
From: Stone, Charlotte P
Subject: Breaking News!!!

Veronica,

I ran the data and it is even worse than the preliminary analysis showed. All in all, women aren't doing as well as men are on the new drug. Right now, the younger women don't look that much different from the younger men. But if you compare the older women to either the older OR younger men (or both combined), the older women are doing much worse. Their depression symptoms aren't getting better AND they are having more side effects, especially sleep disturbances. This really doesn't look good. We have 189 subjects at this point, so the fact that the differences are this extreme in a sample that is this small could spell disaster – this drug may never be marketable. I don't think an antidepressant that worked only for men would fly financially, but I don't know. I will tell Pete. We'll see what happens. Like I think I said, this is not good news, I almost wish that I didn't know.

How did I ever pick this topic for my dissertation?

Yes, you are right about Alexis and Lauren, they are great playmates. They watch TV or use Lauren's computer some of the time they're together, but most of the time they are engaged in some sort of imaginative play, like kids used to be! Yesterday, it sounded like they were acting out "The Princess and the Pea." Frequently, they act out something from school or a story that they've both read.

I'm going to get carry-out from the Ethiopian restaurant just around the corner for dinner. I think I'm entitled to a break from the kitchen when I have to study this much. Of course, it's difficult on the budget, but I think I've got to invest in myself a little bit here and there, you know?

Take care – Charlotte

To: Stone, Charlotte P
Date: Tuesday, January 20
From: Hansen, V
Subject: Re: Breaking News!!

Wow, Charlotte...

This stuff you've found, it could be really important. When will you tell Pete? I feel really excited and nervous for you, I think. Be careful.

Of course, it goes without saying that I will not tell anyone without your permission. I know that I probably don't even have to say that to you, but I did want you to hear it from me.

I'm going out with my friend Julie to a little bar around the corner from me. We used to do this at least once a month, but since I've met Van, we haven't done it for a while. We'll sit there for an hour or so and talk. There are a fair number of regulars there that should recognize us – it hasn't been that long! It is probably better for my health that I don't go that often, too many smokers hanging around outside the door! I'll be washing my hair within 10 minutes of returning from that place. Plus, I only wear older, washable clothes that can go straight into the washer. The place is really kind of a dive!

Like I said – please be careful.

Veronica

To: Stone, Peter E
Date: Tuesday, January 20
From: Stone, Charlotte P
Subject: Need to discuss

Hi Pete,

Hope that things are going well for you. I need to speak with you after the meeting tomorrow. Do you think you can duck over to Schultz's after? This is strictly business, not about Lauren or anything to do with our family. It can be brief, if you need it to be.

Charlotte

To: Stone, Charlotte P
Date: Wednesday, January 21
From: Stone, Peter E
Subject: Re: Need to discuss

Hi Charlotte,

Sure – what's up??

Pete

To: Stone, Peter E
Date: Wednesday, January 21
From: Stone, Charlotte P
Subject: Re: Need to discuss

Hi Pete,

It has to do with the project and also with my dissertation topic. I'll explain more tomorrow.

Charlotte

To: Stone, Charlotte P
Date: Wednesday, January 21
From: Stone, Peter E
Subject: Re: Need to discuss

OK, I'll see you tomorrow. You really have my curiosity up.

Pete

To: Hansen, V
Date: Wednesday, January 21
From: Stone, Charlotte P
Subject: Re: Breaking News!!

Hi Veronica,

Thanks for your concern. I will be careful. So far, all I have done is let Pete know that I need to meet with him, and he is agreeable. I think I will set up an appointment with Dr. Fleming for early next week. That way, I can discuss whatever seems applicable with her, too. I am supposed to meet with her several times a month, anyway.

How was your "dive excursion?" I think I'm about due to go to a dive...I've been to precious few in my lifetime. Except for the smokers, it is probably a good thing to have a place to go to where you can relax and chat with friends.

OK, I need to hit the books seriously, right now. The qualifying exam is looming pretty close on the horizon. I'll be glad when it is safely in the past.

Charlotte

To: Hansen, V
Date: Thursday, January 22
From: Stone, Charlotte P
Subject: Re: Breaking News!!

Veronica,

Oh, my!! Oh, my, my, MY!!!!

My meeting with Pete –

The meeting (group research meeting at SomaRx) actually went pretty well, and it was shorter than most. People were nice to me and Pete was polite and attentive in front of the group, which I appreciated. It was one of those situations where you're still getting things, i.e., work on the new antidepressant project, back together after the holidays. The meeting was a formal way of remembering where we were prior to December 25.

Afterwards, we headed over to Schultz's, and Pete got a piece of pie and I had some coffee. The place was fairly quiet as it was the middle of the afternoon. I told Pete what I had found without too much introduction. I mean, that's my style, just saying what is on my mind pretty directly. I thought he was going to choke on his food after I told him about the trends in the data. He started sputtering and his face turned bright red. He put his fork down and looked away from me. Then he turned back to me and said: "Who do you think you are? You're not a statistician! You're not a senior level researcher! You're not even a junior level researcher! You are some insignificant graduate student that SomaRx is allowing on this project as a favor to Dr. Fleming, due to her previous work for SomaRx. Before you say ANYTHING to ANYBODY you had better make DAMNED SURE that you are right. SomaRx has a LOT of MONEY riding on this drug. They can't afford to let your amateur analysis get out if it is not true."

I asked how it could NOT be true. He said because I may have run the stats incorrectly. I replied that I got the data from the SomaRx biostatisticians, and I used a simple program to run the analysis so far. It isn't rocket science. It seems pretty clear that the drug isn't working for the older women. Pete was silent.

So I asked him what he thought I should do. He said, "I don't know. Let me think about it. I'll call you." I had to leave at this point to pick up Lauren. I wondered if Pete would come with me so we could continue the discussion, but he did not. So here I am, more confused than ever.

But don't worry, I'm "being careful."

Charlotte

To: Stone, Charlotte P
Date: Thursday, January 22
From: Hansen, V
Subject: Re: Breaking News!!

Charlotte,

I don't know what to tell you. This sounds serious. And if you ever need a place to stay because you don't feel safe, you can come to my place. That sounds overly dramatic in a way, but still, if you ever feel you need to take me up on it, do not hesitate. I can even get you a key, if necessary.

Now I'm the one who seems to have the life that is not very exciting. But that will likely change. Things are picking up on the mercy killing case. Van and I will need to continue our interviewing when he gets back from that conference.

If I were you, I would just continue on with things "as usual" until your meeting with Dr. Fleming. Keep me posted.

Veronica

To: Hansen, V
Date: Friday, January 23
From: Stone, Charlotte P
Subject: Re: Breaking News!!

Hi Veronica,

Well, I am very thankful for my "day job" here in Dr. Fleming's office and my need to study for quals. They are giving my life a sense of normality since my conversation with Pete yesterday. I just keep focusing on the task at hand, minute by minute. I don't know what else to do. I keep hoping that the phone will ring, and that it will be Pete and he will have a way to make this "all better."

Why does life have to be so complicated? I don't know. I even looked up the names of several of the chaplains here on campus. Did you know that aside from the hospital chaplains, the campus itself has two: one Protestant, one Catholic. Even though I am not Catholic, I would rather go to him. I think that he will protect me more or something. I have their phone numbers in the back of my date book and in my desk drawer, just in case. It makes me feel more secure, for some reason.

Tonight, Pete is coming to pick up Lauren. That should be interesting. We'll see how it goes.

Well, let's talk about you for a moment. How is your day going? Are you and Van going to do something fun before he has to leave for the forensics seminar? At least the weather is nice, for January. Whatever you do, have fun!

Charlotte

To: Stone, Charlotte P
Date: Friday, January 23
From: Hansen, V
Subject: Re: Breaking News

Hi Charlotte,

Van and I are going out tonight, but more about that in a minute. Call me over-reactive, or overprotective, or whatever, but be careful. Tell me how it goes with Pete. I'm worried. Something is nagging at me. I'm not sure what it is, but something seems wrong with this picture...besides what you are finding out about the drug, I mean.

Van and I are going over to the east side of the state to interview another nurse about the mercy killing case. Then, we're going to go out to eat with another couple that Van has known forever, something to do with one of the first cases that he has ever been involved with. He makes friends with a lot of the victims, or victim's family members, after a case is over. It seems to be true whether he is working for the defense or the prosecution.

Call or email me after Pete stops by to get Lauren.

Veronica

To: Hansen, V
Date: Friday, January 23
From: Stone, Charlotte P
Subject: Pete

Hi Veronica,

Pete was just here. He was pretty low key. He asked me if I had double-checked the numbers again. I told him no, not since we talked. It wasn't necessary since I had already checked and rechecked them. He asked me what I was going to do, and I said I wasn't sure. I asked him if he had any suggestions. He didn't. So, that was about it. I didn't tell him about my meeting with Dr.

Fleming on Monday. For some reason, I thought I'd not say anything about it, at least until it was over.

Lauren was glad to see her Dad, so we didn't discuss it any further. He just said something about his parents, and how they had planned to take Lauren to a movie on Saturday. I reminded him about watching Lauren on next Friday night due to the wedding and he said "Of course." He didn't ask anything more about specifics, and I didn't volunteer any information. So, all systems are "Go!" for the wedding next weekend. That's all that happened. Have a good time with Van after your interview is over!

Charlotte

To: Stone, Charlotte P
Date: Friday, January 23
From: Hansen, V
Subject: Re: Pete

I feel a little better now since Pete seems pretty "normal" in his behavior. I'll email you tomorrow sometime.

Veronica

To: Stone, Charlotte P
Date: Saturday, January 24
From: Hansen, V
Subject: Re: Pete

Hi Charlotte,

Hope your Saturday is going okay so far and that you are able to get some studying done.

My evening yesterday was interesting. We (Van and I) actually interviewed two other nurses related to the mercy killing case. We interviewed them separately. Both are female; one is in her early thirties and the other is 65. Neither one is working for the same hospital where the incident took place at this time. We'll thoroughly check into their backgrounds, but they both are employed by different places now, and both appear to have good employment histories. They also sound reliable. It is unlikely that they currently keep in touch with each other.

There were some minor differences in their stories, but due to the amount of time that has passed, that's not unusual. Basically, the stories meshed. One of them was sitting with the family of the alleged victim at the time of the incident and the other was with the MD who was actively working on the patient. The family was in an adjacent area, and the nurse who was with them (the older one) could hear a little of what was going on, but not everything...only if the voices were raised. The younger nurse, the MD, and a respiratory tech were with the patient, and the nursing supervisor also got involved at some point (we've already spoken with her.) I'll tell you more the next time we meet. If you want to know more about the case at the time, you can search for the MD's name. The case was in all of the state papers following the incident. The MD did have legal charges filed at the time. I think the family is now considering some further legal action, due to withheld evidence or something. And they may be right about that!

After the interviews, Van and I went to this little "Mom and Pop" local bar/restaurant place that he always goes to when he is in that neck of the woods. The "Mom" looks like she is past retirement age and still cooks every night the place is open (five nights a week). I guess the "Pop" is now in a nursing home, but the son and daughter also work there. The food was not fancy, but it was very good. The friends of Van were a charming couple. Even though their son was violently killed, they have put that behind them with a great attitude and forgiveness toward the killer, who was "strung out" (as they put it) on drugs at the time. They said it took a lot of time to get to the point of forgiveness.

Well, I've procrastinated long enough! I need to hit the shower, then get to the grocery store. My cupboards are looking kind of bare.

Take care – Veronica

To: Hansen, V
Date: Saturday, January 24
From: Stone, Charlotte P
Subject: Saturday Doldrums

Hi Veronica,

Yep, I have been able to study...perhaps too well! I now feel kind of restless and bored, so I guess it is time to change activities for a while.

Since Lauren isn't here, I slept about an hour later than usual, then got up, made coffee and hit the books for a couple of hours. Then I went for a walk, came back and showered, and hit the books for a couple more hours, taking a quick break for lunch. Then I studied for about another hour. I'm amazed, quite frankly, that I have been able to concentrate for that long. But let's face it, I'm taking quals soon, so I have to!!

I am also amazed that I've been able to put my concern about the data on the "back burner." But again, maybe it is a matter of having to do that. I can't let that issue interfere with the exam. Since this break-up with Pete, I have been doing better with not letting personal issues interfere with other things. I guess I've been around long enough now to realize that life goes on, no matter what. I think part of that is a little anger too; I'm not going to let HIS actions interfere with MY goals!

I think your Friday evening sounds like it was pretty interesting. I may search for the MD's name in a little bit to find out more. Like I said, I need a little break from studying. I think I will go to the grocery in a little bit, too. I need to start the laundry. Then I'll go back to the studying in a few hours. I'll try to put in another two-hour session today before I go to bed. There is a movie on tonight that I'd like to watch, so I may do that as my last activity of the day.

Enjoy what is left of your Saturday – Charlotte

To: Stone, Charlotte P
Date: Sunday, January 25
From: Hansen, V
Subject: Sunday AM

Hi Charlotte,

Did you watch your movie? Hopefully, you had time to do something relaxing. You know what they say, "all work and no play!" I need to type up some reports today from the interviews I did with Van on Friday. That will probably take a good four hours or so. I'm going to pop a DVD or two in while I do that. . .things I've already seen. I find that works well for me, I need the background noise or something.

Then I'm going to take Robyn to the bookstore. She's ready for another Nancy Drew! I'm letting her pick one out as a reward for helping me out with some housecleaning chores last week.

Have a good one – Veronica

To: Hansen, V
Date: Sunday, January 25
From: Stone, Charlotte P
Subject: Sunday PM

Hi Veronica,

Well, I put the books away, at least for the remainder of the weekend! I'll go get Lauren in about an hour. Then I'll spend some time with her before she needs to get ready for bed. Then, maybe I'll read a trashy novel or magazine until I'm sleepy.

I got lots of studying done this weekend, plus all of the household stuff that was necessary. I feel ready for quals. Of course, I'm a little nervous, too. But I think I'm as prepared as anyone could be. I should do okay.

I'll be relieved to meet with Dr. Fleming tomorrow. I'll get this issue off my chest and into her hands. It still strikes me as strange that Pete hasn't offered any more thoughts on the situation. Maybe he will have some ideas this evening.

Oh, yeah...by the way, Max called me this PM. We chatted for about a half hour. He said he's looking forward to next Friday night. Hmm.

Well, I'm going for a short walk, then I'll pick up Lauren. Enjoy your evening.

Charlotte

To: Stone, Charlotte P
Date: Monday, January 26
From: Hansen, V
Subject: Sending Good Thoughts

Hi Charlotte,

Yep, I really am sending good thoughts your way. I hope all is going, or went, well when you talk(ed) with Dr. Fleming. Did Pete say anything when you picked up Lauren last evening?

Today has been a zoo here. Liz, my histrionic co-worker, claimed she was distracted by having her desk moved a couple of inches to accommodate a new file cabinet. She says this move keeps her more in line with the door, which prevents her from working, because she sees people walking by and she can't "tune it out." She has more excuses than a kid when it comes to reasons for being unable to work. I'm about ready to lose it and tell her off! But, I think I'll be able to keep my cool. Van advises me to just ignore her, and I think that is truly the better way to deal with her manipulative personality!

I did get those reports done for Van over the weekend. Now they will go to the defense team. Personally, I would not want to be the MD under scrutiny in this case. I think something went wrong here, and probably more details will come to light. Van and I have yet to talk with the family members who were called in that night when their

loved one died. That will be next on our list as far as actual
interviews go.

Anyhow, let me know how your meeting with Dr. Fleming goes. I'm
anxious to hear.

Veronica

To: Hansen, V
Date: Monday, January 26
From: Stone, Charlotte P
Subject: Report

Hi Veronica,

Well, thanks for your concern. I met with Dr. Fleming. I feel
somewhat better because she is going to take some action. She told
me that the data that I have been getting from the stats people is
"lumped together." SomaRx is actually studying three doses of the
drug, and I'm getting the results of all three together. So, there is the
potential that the women on one dose may be doing better than
those on other higher doses. She will have them look into it. At least,
it's off my plate for now. I feel like I can breathe a little easier.

Interestingly, Pete said nothing about this last evening when I
picked up Lauren. He is usually a problem-solving, "take charge"
kind of guy, but when he perceives that there is nothing that he can
do, that he is truly out of his league, he'll go into complete denial.
I've only seen this happen a couple of times. Once it happened when
I was pregnant with Lauren and I had some symptoms of preterm
labor at seven months. I was scared. I think Pete was, too, but he
went into this distant, mechanical mode. At the time I felt like he

didn't care, which panicked me even more at the time. Now I know it is his way of feeling both scared and helpless. When I saw him last night, he was pleasant, but pretty mechanical. I reminded him that I would be bringing Lauren over on Friday night, and he said that he and his folks were looking forward to it.

Well, I need to get back to work. I'm glad my meeting with Dr. Fleming is over and that something will be done. In the meantime, it's "business as usual" for me. Take care!

Charlotte

To: Stone, Charlotte P
Date: Tuesday, January 27
From: Hansen, V
Subject: Feeling Lonely

Hi Charlotte,

Van left yesterday PM for his forensics seminar. We're so used to seeing each other every couple of days, so this is going to be different. Of course, we'll be in touch by phone and by email. But I'll know that he is farther away, and for some reason, that makes me feel really lonely. He gets back on Saturday around 3:30 PM. I am going to pick him up at the terminal and then we're going to go for an early dinner at that fancy French restaurant that is near the airport. I haven't been there since I was married, and THAT was a LONG time ago! Anyhow, I'm keeping my sights on Saturday. It can't get here fast enough.

In the meantime, I am going to work on those reports concerning the interviews on the mercy killing case. Originally, the case didn't go to trial. The MD involved went before the medical board and had his license revoked for 6 months. Then he had to have one year of supervision, together with 300 hours of community service. Then it was back to "business as usual," his license was reinstated without any further restrictions. I guess the point I'm trying to make here is that he can still go to trial. There's no statute of limitations on murder! And that is what it is starting to sound like to me. Of course, keep everything I say confidential. Van and I will interview the family members of the deceased when I get back.

So, another couple of days of studying for you, and then the exam! Are you nervous about it?

I'm going to pop a DVD into the player and have it as "background" while I work on these reports. It's *Something's Gotta Give*, one of my favorites. I think I could recite it from beginning to end without any mistakes!

Take care – Veronica

To: Hansen, V
Date: Tuesday, January 27
From: Stone, Charlotte P
Subject: Invitation

Veronica,

OK. I got another "nastygram" in my work email. This one called me "an HIV whore" and told me to "exit science altogether before someone eats you alive." Yes, I feel threatened...but maybe not too much. I have the feeling that the sender is far, far away. "HIV whore" is not an expression that I've ever heard before. But still, it is vicious and nasty. Who could hate me this much? I am doing nothing wrong. I am reporting what I am finding. What else can I do? But, because of the viciousness, I let IT know, and this time the campus police were called. The message didn't directly indicate a threat to harm, at least not from the sender, there was just the threat from an ambiguous "someone." However, now the police know, and that helps me feel a little more secure,

I'm sure the time won't go by fast enough for you. You and Van seem to have quite "the thing" going on between you...and you seem perfect for each other in many ways. He'll miss you, too.

I think I've studied about as much as I can study, given my frame of mind. I'm not one for last-minute cramming. I'll do a review of the outline I made today and tomorrow. That's it. As I said over the weekend, I think I've done a good job of preparing. And I'm determined that my email enemies will NOT derail me from my goal.

Which brings me to the invitation – would you like to come over and have dinner with Lauren and me tomorrow evening? I'll make something easy but good. Cooking will be good therapy for me, I will need something to keep me occupied the night before I take the exam and also to make things seem homey and safe. Making a nice little dinner will do just that. And maybe it will help the time go by a little faster for you, too. I know that you have your project to work on, so you can stay as short or as long as you would like. Lauren usually does her homework right after dinner, so we'll have some time to talk, if you want to. Just let me know.

Charlotte

To: Stone, Charlotte P
Date: Wednesday, January 28
From: Stone, Peter E
Subject: Just checking

Hi Charlotte,

What time will you be dropping Lauren off on Friday? Or, would you rather have me pick her up after work? Just let me know. Oh yeah – what time will you pick her up after the wedding? Let me know.

Pete

To: Stone, Peter E
Date: Wednesday, January 28
From: Stone, Charlotte P
Subject: Re: Just checking

Pete,

If you could pick Lauren up after work, that would be great. I'll pick her up around midnight, if that is okay. I'll send her sleeping bag with her. The reception is at the Mansion on the college campus, and they limit receptions there to five hours maximum. So, I should be ready to pick her up around midnight to 12:30.

Thanks. Charlotte

To: Stone, Charlotte P
Date: Wednesday, January 28
From: Hansen, V
Subject: Re: Invitation

Charlotte,

I would love to come to dinner! Is it okay if I come right after work? That would get me there around 4:30. We'll have some time to gab and I'll still have time to work on the reports after I get home.

And okay, here is something that I just have to say. Maybe at great risk, because I don't want to threaten our friendship – but I also think it would be wrong not to say it.

Do you ever wonder if Pete is one...or both...of your mysterious email correspondents?

For one thing, it would explain the personal knowledge about your hair color and the silver dress in addition to your research and the concerns about SomaRx. It may even be an attempt to derail your success at the qualifying exams. You hear and read true crime stories like this all of the time, that the criminal is someone close to the victim. And, of course, I've seen it and also heard Van talk about other cases where this is true.

I realize this may come as a shock. But I had to let you know what I was thinking. I don't want you to get hurt, that's my bottom line. I am your friend.

Veronica

To: Hansen, V
Date: Wednesday, January 28
From: Stone, Charlotte P
Subject: Re: Invitation

Veronica –

I am not angry. I've actually considered...but discarded...the thought that Pete may be involved with the emails. But every time that I think of that, I think of when he and I sat at the Medici together, discussing our impressions regarding the sick babies and their care. And that person that I sat with then, could never, ever do those things. Pete may be confused. But he is not evil. But I do appreciate your concern for my safety.

As far as your RSVP to my little dinner, what you've proposed would be fine. I started the roast in the slow cooker this AM and it will be ready whenever we're ready to eat it. So come on over whenever you want! I'll be picking Lauren up at 3:30 and should be home by 4:00.

Looking forward to it!

Charlotte

To: Stone, Charlotte P
Date: Wednesday, January 28
From: Strong, James Y
Subject: Re: Query: Central College Days??

Hello! How are things going? I thought about you today when I got some information about a new graduate program at Central College. Are you surviving the Midwest winter so far?

All the best

Jim

James Y Strong, PhD
Dean, School of Science
South Central State

To: Strong, James Y
Date: Wednesday, January 28
From: Stone, Charlotte P
Subject: Re: Query: Central College Days??

Hello – things are going pretty well. I take my qualifying exam tomorrow. Maybe I'll know better then! Thanks for asking. CS

To: Stone, Charlotte P
Date: Wednesday, January 28
From: Hansen, V
Subject: Thanks

Hi Charlotte,

I'm just about ready to turn in for the night. I've got about 2/3 of the interview data typed up into reports re: the mercy killing case. I'll have it done by the time Van gets back from his conference. I talked with him this evening. He is learning a lot and reconnecting with old friends. He told me briefly about a medical forensics seminar he attended yesterday evening. Sounded very interesting. He will bring home all of the handouts and make a copy for me.

Thanks so much for inviting me for dinner. I haven't had a home-cooked meal like that for at least a month. Most of the time, it is when Allen is in a cooking mood and usually the menu is Italian in that case. The roast that you made and all of the trimmings were great! It was fun to talk with Lauren, too; she is a delightful young lady!

You have the best (or the most) intuition of anyone I know. So – I'll respect your opinion about Pete. Just be careful!

I know that you will do well tomorrow AM – get a good night's sleep!

Veronica

To: Hansen, V
Date: Thursday, January 29
From: Stone, Charlotte P
Subject: Over!

Hi Veronica,

Well, my exams are over and I survived. I was challenged, but I think I did well. Of course, you always think of things you could have done differently afterwards. But overall, I'm happy with how I did. I will forget about it until next week when I meet with my committee and have the oral defense. I'm now in my office. I'm going to go and get some lunch in a few minutes. Then I'll come back here and work for a couple of hours before I go and get Lauren. When I say "work," I will probably just do some routine tasks, like filing. After an experience like this, I find it difficult to concentrate on anything really demanding for a while. Anyhow, now I can relax and enjoy the wedding this weekend. Hope your day is going well. I'll probably write more later. Charlotte

To: Stone, Charlotte P
Date: Thursday, January 29
From: Hansen, V
Subject: Re: Over!

Congratulations! I decided to "get away" from the unit for lunch. Right now I'm in the hospital library. Things are really kind of uncomfortable at work today. One of the MDs is on the rampage. She gets like this from time to time and decides something (or someone) needs to be corrected right now. I'll let my boss deal with it, that's why she gets paid the big bucks!

Enjoy your afternoon!

Veronica

To: Hansen, V
Date: Thursday, January 29
From: Stone, Charlotte P
Subject: Re: Over!

Hi Veronica,

I did enjoy my afternoon. I filed and tidied my little office. It gave me a nice, "loose ends tied up" feeling. I picked up Lauren and made us an easy little dinner from yesterday's leftovers. Then I treated myself to some "junk TV" for an hour, something I rarely get to do during the academic year.

I took the dress I wore on my birthday to the cleaners around the corner earlier this week. It will be ready tomorrow for the wedding. I wish I had time to get my hair done but I don't. I need to put in a full day's work tomorrow. So, I'll do my hair myself. It is really easy to get it looking nice with the hair ornament that I bought to go with the dress. A person at work is lending me a warm wrap to take in case I get cold wearing a sleeveless dress – she said the Mansion can be drafty in spots in the winter. (I did tell you that the Mansion on the college campus is where the reception is, right?) I'm anxious to see what it is like on the inside. In fact, this whole experience is as close to a "no stress" wedding as a person can get in this lifetime. I like Max, but he is definitely only a friend, I'm not trying to impress him. I don't even know either family involved in the wedding. I don't have to get a gift, that's Max's responsibility. So, like I said – a no-stress wedding, from my point of view.

Also, Max called this PM, it was a brief conversation to clarify when he would pick me up. I appreciate his consideration in addressing that little item on the day before.

So, you've made it through the week...almost. Only one more day without Van. Are you still going to the French restaurant? Should be fun. I want to hear all of the details about the food there.

OK, all of a sudden, I'm exhausted. Must be the "let-down" after today's exam! Have a good evening.

Charlotte

To: Stone, Charlotte P
Date: Friday, January 30
From: Hansen, V
Subject: Re: Over!

Hi Charlotte,

Sounds like your evening last night was relaxing, and that is probably rare for you on a weeknight! We all need a little "mental oasis" now and then. You certainly deserve it – you've been working hard and put in a lot of studying over the weekend.

I have missed Van very much! We are in contact almost every day, just like when he is home, but knowing that he is 1000 miles away makes it different somehow! I am very, very anxious to see him. I'm looking forward to our "date." The food should be great, but most of all, it will be something special to do together. At some point during the next week, I will make copies of everything he brings home from the seminar and go through it all. We make good partners, I think. I love this type of work and obviously, so does he. When I can retire from nursing (which won't be anytime soon; I need to work myself out of debt first!) I can see us working together on cases until both of us can no longer drive. Maybe people will write books about us in the future! Ha! The geriatric detectives!

Well, tonight is your "reward night" after studying so hard. Like you said, a no-stress wedding. A rare event, indeed. I'll look forward to hearing the details. Enjoy!

Veronica

Part Four
February

To: Hansen, V
Date: Sunday, February 1
From: Stone, Charlotte P
Subject: The details

Hi Veronica,

I hope your weekend with Van was wonderful. What was it that I said about a "no stress" wedding? Whatever it was, I take it back.

Everything started out all right. Pete came and picked up Lauren as promised. She was looking forward to it...had her favorite doll and her sleeping bag ready to go. I picked up my dress from the cleaner's. I had the stole from my co-worker. I did my own hair and it looked fine. Max picked me up on time. He wore a black suit that almost looked like a tux. He smelled great, too. I made a comment about it. He said something like, "Well, when you've been working with puking babies all day, you need to do something about it!" (Remember, I told you that his specialty is kids with colic.) So anyhow, the evening got off to a good start.

The wedding itself was classy. The ceremony was at 7 PM. It was in the "chapel" on the St. Catherine College campus, which is actually bigger than a lot of churches. It was decorated nicely. The bride and bridal party looked sophisticated. The dresses were elegant but simple in design. The bridesmaids wore deep burgundy velvet and carried deep red roses and white carnations. The bride carried a mixture of red and white roses in a very unique and beautiful arrangement. The ceremony was well under an hour, and then everyone walked down the drive to The Mansion where the bridal party had formed their receiving line and food and drink was available immediately. Within an hour, the cake was cut and the band was playing and people were dancing. The bar included free wine and beer, and there was also a cash bar for other drinks. People were drinking, but no one got obnoxious. The band was pretty good. In general, people seemed to be having a good time. The parents of both the bride and groom were very gracious people and also seemed to be enjoying themselves. Max was very attentive and introduced me to everyone. His family seems close-knit and nice.

At about 11:15, the bridal couple came down the stairs after changing into their "going away" clothes. It made for a dramatic exit. After they took off, people started to leave. Max and I left about 11:40. Here's where the problems began. He (evidently) thought that he was going to be spending the night at my place! He ASSUMED this. I guess the fact that Lauren was at her dad's place, and NOT at our apartment with a sitter, confirmed this idea in his reptilian male brain or something! So, after arriving at the curb in front of my building, he looked at me and said something like: "Are you going to officially invite me in?" I said "No, I'm a little late for picking up Lauren, so I need to get over to her dad's." I expected him to then say something like, "OK, I'll take a rain check" or something that would fit the usual social banter.

Wow, was I surprised. He got really angry. I mean really, really angry. His face got very red. He grabbed the back of my neck and pulled me across the seat and started kissing me hard, in a very strange way. I friend of mine in high school had told me that one of her boyfriends "kissed like a rock" and I thought "this must be what she meant." My coat wasn't buttoned, and he grabbed my breast. I started to cry; I think it was because this was so unexpected. I thought we would be saying our civilized "thank yous" and "good nights" and that would be the end of the evening. Somehow, I regained my composure and said, "Max, I need to leave." I got out of the car and walked quickly to mine, which was only a few cars away. I got in, and drove away. I felt kind of shaky, but made it to Pete's parents' home without any problem. I checked to see if Max was following me, but he did not.

Once at Pete's, I knocked on the door. I could see the light was on in the living room, and I saw Pete's silhouette in the easy chair. He opened the door. I could see that Lauren was still awake. She was lying on her sleeping bag. They had been watching some old black-and-white movie together. She said "Mommie!" when I walked in, and Pete smiled. He said that they had had fun together. His parents had gone to bed about a half-hour before, but they had all played games for most of the evening. Pete asked me in, and poured me a cup of tea that he said he had just made. It tasted wonderful. I debated about whether to ask him to follow us home, but I decided against it. I had my cell phone. If anything didn't "look right" when Lauren and I got back, I wouldn't stop, but call Pete at that point. Lauren got her things together, and we got ready to leave. Pete then asked me about the data. I told him that I had brought it to the attention of Dr. Fleming, and it was in her hands now. He just said "OK" and looked kind of relieved.

So Lauren and I came home without incident. I felt shaky again once outside the apartment. I think what scared me was the fact that I "didn't see it coming" in addition to the anger in Max's voice and behavior. He had two drinks all evening. In no way would I consider him drunk. There were no "suggestions" made earlier in the evening. But, I guess we both had a script in mind for how the evening would end, and they were very, very different. What continues to amaze me is how Max thought spending the night was a "given." That just floors me. The forcefulness in his actions was the most unnerving, though, far more so than the sexual advances themselves. I was glad I was able to exit the car without problem.

Well, Veronica, you were right! About the "no pressure" line. About guys and weddings! From now on, I'm taking you as chaperone. (Only kidding.) I'm not doing this type of thing (I guess you call it dating) again for a while, if ever. I really wanted to talk to someone Saturday AM, but I didn't want to put a damper on your day with Van. So – even though it was Saturday, I decided to call Alejandro and see if he had an opening for a haircut. Because, like I said, he's a good listener. And I needed a cut, anyway.

He really didn't have an opening, but stayed an extra hour instead. He said he didn't have any plans to go out of town this weekend, which he frequently has during the warmer months. Pete's mom was available for Lauren, and Alejandro's salon is less than a mile from their place. So, I went in at three. He cut my hair and I told him my troubles. I didn't go into great detail, just said something about having a "no pressure date" that turned out to have "pressure" anyway. He said, "Oh yeah, yeah – there's always some kind of pressure. It sounds like this guy thought that you would be an easy mark." (Thank goodness, he didn't say '"easy lay"...I think I would have lost it if he had). "And he's a doctor, he may not have too many women turn him down." (Which may be true...how would I know?) Anyhow, it was good to get it off my chest, plus get the male perspective. Then Alejandro asked if I would be interested in any "referrals" from some of his male clients. (!) He said he knew some men that were "nice guys" who would "treat me right" and would be "very interested" in dating someone like me. One is a computer programmer and one works for a pharmaceutical/biotech company (NOT SomaRx).

I told him thanks, but I think I need to stay out of the dating scene right now. I'm not really interested in finding someone. This whole wedding thing – I thought I was doing it as a favor for Max because he couldn't find anyone else. I guess I didn't realize the extent of the "favors" he thought I would give him!

Anyhow, I felt better after talking with Alejandro (I always do...who needs therapy?) Plus, I had a great looking haircut which also helped to lift my spirits.

You'll never guess what just happened. Someone just knocked at my door. I looked through the peephole and it was Max! I'm not even sure how he got in the building, I definitely didn't buzz him in. I told him to GO AWAY (not opening the door). He said he was sorry. I said "OK, then leave!" He did. I watched him drive away from my bedroom window. Men! I think I am through with them for a while.

This is the longest email that I have written for a long, long time. Thanks for "listening." I'll be anxious to hear how your weekend went.

Charlotte

To: Stone, Charlotte P
Date: Sunday, February 1
From: Hansen, V
Subject: Re: The Details

Hi Charlotte,

Well, it is 10 PM, later than I usually check email, but that is an indication of how my weekend has gone. Mine went very, very well. The French restaurant was fantastic. I have a little knowledge of French food, since I've been to Paris once, but the wait staff is very, very helpful in assisting you to choose items that you will like, even if you are unfamiliar with the cuisine. The quality of the food was excellent, and they truly make it a "dining experience." Van had a lot to tell me about the seminar. I filled him in regarding the reports of the mercy killing case. I told him to read the reports himself, too. Some things kind of "clicked" for me in a different way after reading the written word. Anyhow, Van and I had a lot of catching up to do, so we spent a lot of time together this weekend, more than we usually do.

Well, I'm sorry your "stress-free" wedding ended on a sour note. Like I said, that "no pressure" line always raises my index of suspicion! Groping you – that was definitely over the line. However, if he is at all civilized, I would bet that Max realizes that and his "I'm sorry" was genuine. He probably really likes you more than he's letting on. How you deal with this is up to you. If you want to stay away from social situations with men, well...that's one way to deal with it.

I would agree that Alejandro is a good listener and a good story teller. I think it is interesting that he had two people that he could recommend for you "on the spot." Maybe he does a lot of matchmaking. In his line of work, he probably has a good idea of who would be compatible with whom!

I need to get to bed. Five AM rolls around quickly! And the stress level at work seemed to be escalating last week, partly due to rumors of a corporate reorganization that was getting the MDs all riled up. Maybe it will be calmer this week! Take care, and keep your chin up!

Veronica

To: Stone, Charlotte P
Date: Monday, February 2
From: Strong, James Y
Subject: Exams

Hi! How were your examinations? I hope they went well. You probably impressed your readers!

All the best

Jim

James Y Strong, PhD
Dean, School of Science
South Central State

To: Strong, James Y
Date: Monday, February 2
From: Stone, Charlotte P
Subject: Re: Exams

Thank you. I do think the examination went well. I think that I was very prepared, and pretty relaxed for a qualifying exam taker. That helped a lot!

Charlotte

To: Stone, Charlotte P
Date: Monday, February 2
From: Strong, James Y
Subject: Re: Exams

Hello!

Yes, you are correct in saying that being prepared really helps to take the pressure off. I am always amazed at how many students don't seem to understand that! Anyhow, congratulations on completing one important step toward getting your degree.

All the best

Jim

James Y Strong, PhD
Dean, School of Science
South Central State

To: Strong, James Y
Date: Monday, February 2
From: Stone, Charlotte P
Subject: Re: Exams

Thank you. It always amazes me how close some people cut academic corners, too!

Charlotte

To: Hansen, V
Date: Monday, February 2
From: Stone, Charlotte P
Subject: Your weekend

Hi Veronica,

Well, I was glad to know that your weekend went well. In fact, it sounds like it was pretty wonderful. French food, forensics and Van – sounds like a perfect weekend for you!! I'm calmer now. I have to admit, I was pretty shaky after the groping incident. I mean, it's not like I was raped or anything, but there was a hint of anger and out-of-control behavior that was a little scary. Max realizes that I'm sure. Yes, you are probably right that his apology was sincere. But, I'm going to take a <u>giant</u> step backward from dating at this time. I really didn't look at the wedding as a real date anyway, it was a favor – I thought. And, I'm not really interested in any relationships right now. I'm still married, and I'm still interested in re-establishing my relationship with Pete. And here's a thought: maybe Max is the mysterious emailer. He knows my hair color, obviously, but it doesn't explain knowing the color of my dress on the night of my birthday. Maybe he followed me? Or just happened to see me? I guess it could be possible. Anyhow, that display of anger – that's what makes me wonder if it could be him. I'm not going anywhere with him, or meeting him anywhere, anymore.

On a lighter note...yes, you are right, it is kind of cute and interesting that Alejandro had two guys "in mind" for me. I wonder how often that he does the "matchmaking" thing. I'll have to ask him next time.

We have a research meeting on Thursday, and I need to talk with Pete afterwards about money. Remember how I said that when

February rolled around, I'd be needing more money? Well, it is February, and I do need more cash. I used some Christmas gift money to pay the rent for last month, but this month I'll need some help, I think.

Today was pretty much a routine day, EXCEPT Dr. Strong emailed me again. Just very short little messages, as seems to be his "usual." I have to admit that it is kind of fun – and it also seems very safe!

Take care –

Charlotte

To: Stone, Peter E
Date: Monday, February 2
From: Stone, Charlotte P
Subject: Thursday after the meeting

Hi Pete,

Can I meet with you briefly after the research meeting on Thursday? I have a financial concern that I need to discuss. Thanks again for taking care of Lauren last weekend.

Charlotte

To: Stone, Charlotte P
Date: Monday, February 2
From: Stone, Peter E
Subject: Re: Thursday after the meeting

Charlotte,

Yes, I can meet for a few minutes. And I can help you out this month with living expenses, if that is what you need. You've shouldered most the burden so far.

See you Thursday.

Pete

To: Stone, Charlotte P
Date: Monday, February 2
From: Hansen, V
Subject: Re: Your weekend

Charlotte,

Hello and Happy Groundhog Day! Personally, I love that movie with Bill Murray. Sometimes I feel like I am living it! Especially when I wake up to "I've Got You, Babe" on the radio.

My day was pretty routine, too, and I am glad! I was dreading some kind of knock-down, drag-out fight between the MDs and nursing administration on our unit. But today was pretty calm and civil...probably the calm before the storm. I'm sure some kind of disagreement is coming, but I'll take the peace and quiet while it lasts.

Van should be calling me in a little while. We need to work on the mercy killing case and plan our next interviews. Since no charges were filed by the authorities the first time around (the only punishment came from the medical board), I guess they could be filed this time around. I need to ask Van where he thinks that this is all heading.

Tonight, I will research the MD online, and go over everything that I find on the web.

Most of the social workers and other nurses on our unit were pretty quiet today. That is unusual. I guess that we are all counting our blessings, I think everyone knows that the peace and quiet won't last.

Well, the mysterious Dr. Strong...that is interesting! Yes, I can see how he is something of "safe excitement" for you.

Have a good evening – relax! You do deserve it after your exam, you've been working hard, and also have been through a lot of stress. (And I can understand the "raped" feeling. One of our counselors here says "rape isn't about penetration." I think she's right.)

Veronica

To: Hansen, V
Date: Tuesday, February 3
From: Stone, Charlotte P
Subject: Something weird

Hi Veronica,

Another strange thing happened in my work email today. I got a bogus email with an attachment containing a virus. After asking around, many people have experienced that type of thing at one time or another (the virus attachment). But it is the first time for me. Why? The subject line, sender's name and attachment title all contain violent, derogatory comments about women, including the "c word." Who could be doing this? And why is this happening now? And why in my work email, which I would assume would be more secure than my personal email? Like I said, this type of thing has happened to many of my co-workers in the past, but no one else got this particular email today. And most people that I have talked to said that mine looked and sounded nastier than any they have received.

Oh well, I guess there is nothing I can really do about it. Obviously, I won't reply to it. I guess I should delete it. But, I'd rather keep it, because it is "evidence" in case the trend continues, or something. I showed it to our IT people.

How did the sender get my name? Once again I wondered if it could be Max. After all, he has an email account on the same university system. I guess I should just stop worrying about it. I just feel like someone must hate me very much to send something so nasty. However, now that I mention it, I think that Pete told me a while back that tons of nasty emails came through to SomaRx. It took their IT department a while to get them blocked.

I am so naive, at first, I tried to open the attachment. But the "system" wouldn't let me. Thank goodness! It gave me a message that the attachment contained a virus, so it couldn't be opened. I'm very grateful for the built-in protection of our technology.

OK, that is enough about that topic. How did your search engine investigation go concerning your MD suspect? Did you uncover anything interesting? Like I've said, your life seems more intriguing than mine...you're solving a decade-old mystery.

Speaking of Max, I haven't heard anything from him. So, maybe he will just fade away, which is okay with me. I never really have to run into him for any reason, so there shouldn't be any awkward situations.

Well, this is a disjointed, silly email. I hope your day went well and that the calm is lasting on your hospital unit.

Charlotte

To: Stone, Charlotte P
Date: Tuesday, February 3
From: Hansen, V
Subject: Re: Something Weird

Hi Charlotte,

Well, your email did sounds a little disjointed and you do sound a little upset. But I would be, too, if I received such an email. Plus, this comes on top of an upsetting weekend for you, and the stress of your qualifying exams. As Van would say, there are tons of weird people in the world and the internet gives them the anonymity to do a lot of things that they wouldn't otherwise do. Basically, they are perverted cowards (that is MY take on the situation, not Van's). But I do think that Van would agree with me :-D!

Van was going to consult with the prosecutors (actually the present one and the one who was in office at the time of the mercy killing who is now in private practice.) He will tell them what we have found so far and who we still plan to interview. However, right now his clients are the family members of the deceased. They are trying to decide whether or not to file a civil wrongful death suit. However, who knows, it may end up being a lot more than that. I'm sure the MD in question does not know anything about our investigation. He has had nothing to do with the hospital where the incident took place for years, and now practices in Indianapolis. He has a specialty practice that is not likely to put him in contact with people who have life-threatening health problems, and that is good for him and the public, in my opinion. But maybe he deserves to be locked up. Time will tell.

Well, I need to run. I'm meeting Van for a business dinner. I need to bring the reports that are done and we will plan the next move. I love this work! I wish I could do it full time! Unfortunately, I still need a "day job," for health insurance, among other things.

Take care, and let me know if you need anything.

Veronica

To: Hansen, V
Date: Wednesday, February 4
From: Stone, Charlotte P
Subject: Something even weirder

Hi Veronica,

Okay, now I'm really upset! And creeped out, to some extent, but mostly upset. I got a call from Dr. Fleming when I arrived at the office this AM. She wanted to see me. When I got to her office, she told me Dr. Mueller, the big head honcho of the antidepressant project, had requested that I not attend further research meetings and that "perhaps" I'll need to think of a different topic for my dissertation.

Dr. Fleming herself was somewhat apologetic about this development. She said she had only one other student who had used SomaRx study data as part of a dissertation, and there had been no problems. She asked me if I had any questions, and I said no, the message was clear. I was pretty much overwhelmed. I think I just got up and left. I'm still numb, this happened about a half hour ago. My brain is still all tied up with this; it is really difficult for me to concentrate on anything else. What I keep asking myself is: "What does this all MEAN?" And I don't exactly know, other than it sounds serious.

I also got another one of those weird emails in my university email account. This one said: "Think you're a scientist? You're really a stupid bitch. You don't have the faintest clue of how to analyze anything. Give it up." The attachment was entitled "Stupid Bitch with no Brain." Nice. I didn't open that, of course. I showed it to our IT people. No direct threat, although it seems personal. Aimed at me. Now I'm wondering if the weird emails and my removal from the project are related. Someone doesn't like me, that is clear. And why? Because I have a brain? Because I'm trying to scientifically examine something? I'm really not very threatening. I have no legitimate power in the organization for heaven's sake. I'm the lowest on the totem pole, a student. I've even wondered about Dr. Fleming; is she truly my friend and advocate? I'm not sure who I can trust. I still don't think it is Pete, but I can understand why the thought would cross your mind.

I am going to TRY and get some work done. More later.

Charlotte

To: Stone, Charlotte P
Date: Wednesday, February 4
From: Hansen, V
Subject: Re: Something even weirder

Charlotte,

I don't want to sound like an alarmist, or get you more worried. I really think you're safe, but...be careful. You have information that could be damaging to SomaRx. They are asking you to erase your computer, but they can't erase your brain. And you are right – you are low on the totem pole, but "they" (the higher-ups at SomaRx) have no legitimate control over you either, for that very reason. I think that you have someone very, very worried. Maybe more than one someone. I am going to talk to Van about this.

In the meantime, just go about your life. Even if you don't attend the meeting, will you meet with Pete afterwards? Maybe you should try to postpone meeting with him. I'm sure that you can think of another area for your dissertation. It is probably lucky that you haven't officially started on it yet.

I'll write more later. Just be careful.

Veronica

PS – I read somewhere that you should conduct an online search for yourself from time to time, because it lets you know what others can easily find out about you. Maybe you should do that.

To: Stone, Charlotte P
Date: Wednesday, February 4
From: Hansen, V
Subject: Re: Something even weirder

I just got off my cell phone with Van. He agrees with me, best for you to be prudent. As he put it – any time you have the ability to influence someone else's authority or income, people will be watching you. So be careful. If you feel like you can't postpone your meeting with Pete, I would advise you to do it away from SomaRx – not at Schultz's, but in a public place.

Did you do a web search for yourself yet? Let me know when you have read this.

Veronica

To: Hansen, V
Date: Wednesday, February 4
From: Stone, Charlotte P
Subject: Re: Something even weirder

Veronica,

All of a sudden I feel like I am in "Spy vs. Spy" from *Mad Magazine*. Am I the one in white or the one in black?

So, I have followed your advice. I have searched the web for myself. Mostly pretty boring. A few old running times from races a couple of years ago. An abstract I submitted for the research meeting later this month. Some references that are really about other people with the same name. But, here is a strange thing – my name shows up as connected with a porn site. That seems odd. Then here is something else strange. If you search for an image associated with my name, one image shows up: the logo for "Minerva's Voice: The Forum for Wise Women at South Central State, Colorado." It is really just a design incorporating the South Central State crest – or whatever you want to call it. However, I cannot find my name anywhere on the site. It is a huge site, though. It looks similar to the home page associated with my personal email; has various stories, ads, directories, etc. For example, it has about 20 personal or dating sites attached to it, plus realtors, businesses in the campus area...it goes on and on. Some of them are more female oriented, but not all. I cannot find my name anywhere. At least there's no porn!

I think I will email Pete and tell him what has happened. I really do need to talk to him, I need help with February's rent and it is already overdue! More later –

Charlotte

To: Stone, Peter E
Date: Wednesday, February 4
From: Stone, Charlotte P
Subject: Our meeting

Pete,

Hi. As you may have heard by now, I've been banned from the research meeting tomorrow. I may need to find a new dissertation topic. I'm not sure what is going on exactly, other than that Dr. Mueller doesn't want me there. Has he said anything to you about it? I wonder how he feels about you being at the meeting.

Anyhow, I really do need to meet with you tomorrow. Any chance we could meet at another location (not Schultz's), but at the same time? I feel a little strange meeting so close to SomaRx now.

Charlotte

To: Stone, Charlotte P
Date: Wednesday, February 4
From: Stone, Peter E
Subject: Re: Our meeting

Charlotte,

I'm shocked. I knew nothing about forbidding you from attending the research team meeting. I don't know what to say, other than it sounds serious. I had spoken to no one about what you told me.

As far as meeting...yes, I can still do it. But it really works out easier for me if we meet at Schultz's. Otherwise, I'll need to drive somewhere, and that will cut down on the time I have to actually talk with you. The only other alternative, that does not involve driving for me would be to meet here in the plant, at the cafeteria or in my office. I'm assuming that you would not want to do either of those.

Are you upset? I feel bad. I would never have guessed that this would happen.

Pete

To: Stone, Peter E
Date: Wednesday, February 4
From: Stone, Charlotte P
Subject: Re: Our meeting

Hi Pete,

Thanks for your concern. Reading your email made me feel a little better. For some reason, I feel like I got my hand slapped for doing something wrong. But all I have done is begin to collect data for a topic that I had identified and that had been approved. I wasn't that invested in it; I can switch to something else. Veronica acts like I might be in some sort of danger, but, I think that she's over-reacting.

What I need to talk to you about has nothing to do with the research project. It is financial, and won't take long. I would just like to talk to you in person. And with the recent developments, I'd also like you to tell me what is said about me in the meeting, if anything. So let's stick to our usual plan. Actually, you could call me on my cell when the meeting is over, and I'll meet you at Schultz's.

See you then.

Charlotte

To: Stone, Charlotte P
Date: Wednesday, February 4
From: Stone, Peter E
Subject: Re: Our meeting

OK. I'll call you. See you tomorrow.

Pete

To: Stone, Charlotte P
Date: Wednesday, February 4
From: Hansen, V
Subject: Re: Something even weirder

Hi Charlotte,

I don't know what to make of the 'Minerva' thing. It sounds kind of strange, but it could be just a coincidence. Did you have your name in quotes when you searched? If not, well, it just means that the two parts of your name showed up in somewhat close proximity somewhere on the huge site. And "stone" is an ordinary word, too; in addition to being your last name.

I guess that there is no need to panic. Like I said, just be careful and live your life normally. But, if you want, my offer is always open; you and Lauren can always stay here as long as you need to.

When is the oral defense of your qualifying exam?

Veronica

To: Hansen, V
Date: Wednesday, February 4
From: Stone, Charlotte P
Subject: Re: Something even weirder

Veronica,

Cyberspace must be smoking! I don't think I've exchanged this many emails in this short of a time ever! I've never even thought of using instant messaging as it never seemed better than simply calling someone. This is probably the closest I've come to doing it.

I emailed Pete. He has heard nothing about my "banishment." He was surprised. We will still meet tomorrow after the meeting. That's about all to report.

My oral defense of the qualifying exam is Friday, the day AFTER tomorrow. Hopefully, I'll be able to concentrate. If not, I will just explain my lack of ability to think and the reason for it. Dr. Fleming knows anyway, and the others will probably hear via the grapevine beforehand. It may just be good for me to have something to do, so we'll see how the next 24 hours unfold.

The immediate shock and numbness of this situation has worn off. I think I can go back to some routine work now. I'll let you know how it goes tomorrow.

Take care,

Charlotte

To: Hansen, V
Date: Thursday, February 5
From: Stone, Charlotte P
Subject: Re: Post meeting report

Hi Veronica,

Pete and I met. As far as rent money goes, Pete said that he is more than willing to help. He wrote me a check for the full month's rent, right then and there, so that worry is over. I'll worry about March in a few weeks.

Pete also told me that no mention was made about my whereabouts, or my "banishment" from the research meeting today. Now that I think about it, I'm not very surprised at that. I'm pretty low on the totem pole and have no special expertise that would benefit the research team. And it is not unusual for people on the team to miss a meeting or two during the course of a year. People may have even attributed it to the fact that Pete and I are separated.

However, I think my research idea is, or was, a good one. But the information that it is yielding is upsetting to someone. Now what? Do I continue looking at that same general research question (lifestyle habits and depressive symptoms, but NOT with people on SomaRx's new drug), or should I just go off on a different tangent altogether?

Pete was polite and cordial, but somewhat distant during the time we were together. He had a piece of pie, but he just picked at it. I was half tempted to ask him if he was dating anyone, but I thought I'd better leave it alone. I don't think I could handle anymore upsetting news right now, so I'll study for tomorrow's exam instead.

Have a good evening.

Charlotte

To: Stone, Charlotte P
Date: Friday, February 6
From: Strong, James Y
Subject: Re: Exams

I will be in your area for a research summit the week of February 20. Is there any chance we could meet for a quick cup of coffee or something?

All the best

Jim

James Y Strong, PhD
Dean, School of Science
South Central State

To: Hansen, V
Date: Friday, February 6
From: Stone, Charlotte P
Subject: okay, now it's getting really weird

Hi Veronica,

First of all, I just had my oral defense, and it went fine. In some
respects, I guess, it was relatively easy; because everyone said I did a
good job in the written exam, there was very little "defending" that
needed to be done. Also, I think maybe the word had gotten around
about my "banishment," so maybe people did not want to be too
hard on me. I'll take whatever help I can get! I'm glad all of the
exams are over. Now – on to the dissertation! I'm going to give
myself a week or so off. If any ideas come to mind, great; if not, I'll
start going to the library and mulling over potential changes in focus
at that point.

Now – here is the something even weirder...Dr. Strong emailed me
and says he will be in the area soon. He wants to meet, it sounds like
something very brief. "A cup of coffee" is what he said. That means
about 15 minutes to an hour, to me, which I think would be fine.
However, after my recent "no pressure" wedding experience, I'm a
little gun shy. Still, it seems harmless enough. The research summit
that he'll be attending is a real event going on at the university
conference center, and it has a very good reputation. So, I'm sure
that he is coming for that. As I write this, I feel less worried. I think
I'm just paranoid because of everything else that has been going on.

This is Pete's weekend to have Lauren. I will miss having her around, but this will also give me a weekend to do NOTHING, other than just catch up on my laundry and maybe even read a novel – that sounds VERY good right now.

Charlotte

To: Stone, Charlotte P
Date: Friday, February 6
From: Hansen, V
Subject: Recent developments

Hi Charlotte,

I agree that Dr. Strong sounds harmless enough. A cup of coffee is pretty innocent. And he is probably very busy, so a few minutes is probably all that he will have time for. As a "higher-up" in academia, one would assume that he's fairly straightforward. But you could have the university check him out, especially since they've been watching all of the strange events in your email account.

Tonight, Van and I go back to the eastern part of the state to conduct one more interview regarding the mercy killing case. This person was a little hard to find, but thanks to Van's excellent detective work (with my assistance, I might add :-D!) she has been found and is willing to be interviewed. This witness was a family member of another person being treated in the ED of the hospital in question the night of the incident. We view her as a good prospect because she is not employed in health care, so is free of any of the "there but for the grace of God go I" type of feelings that the health care providers we interviewed might have. I'm excited. I think this interview is going to clinch the case!

Well, do you have time for coffee on Sunday, either late AM or in the afternoon? I'll be typing up reports, but I'll have time for a break. It might be a chance for you to debrief or vent. Sounds like we both have a lot going on. Let me know. We could meet at the coffee shop near your church or wherever else you would like.

TAKE CARE!! (I mean it!)

Veronica

To: Strong, James Y
Date: Friday, February 6
From: Stone, Charlotte P
Subject: Re: Exams

Hello. Yes, we could probably come up with a time to meet. I'm usually at the School of Nursing or the Health Sciences Library when I'm not in class. Both are close to the conference center, so I could probably meet for a quick cup of coffee.

Charlotte

To: Stone, Charlotte P
Date: Friday, February 6
From: Strong, James Y
Subject: Re: Exams

Great! I will look forward to meeting you. I am impressed with the health science research that is going on at your institution. As a chemist, I'm more familiar with bench science, but I am really impressed by the innovative health care therapies that are being tested currently. I hope to learn more about them at the summit and bring some ideas back to South Central State.

I'll be in touch again when I know more about my schedule.

All the best

Jim

James Y Strong, PhD
Dean, School of Science
South Central State

**To: Hansen, V
Date: Saturday, February 7
From: Stone, Charlotte P
Subject: Re: Recent Developments**

Hi Veronica,

As far as coffee goes – you're on! How about Sunday at 11AM at the "usual" spot?

I hope your interview panned out – that it was all that you had hoped for.

Dr. Strong says that he is looking forward to meeting me. Hmm. Oh well, something different. I am kind of curious about him. And the university considers him "cleared" as far as security goes.

I am going to the library in a little while. The public library, that is, to look for a book, a novel, a story...something to read for enjoyment over the next week. What a treat!

I'm also going to try and get out and enjoy some of this winter sunshine. It looks kind of nice outside today.

Have a good day. See you tomorrow!

Charlotte

To: Stone, Charlotte P
Date: Saturday, February 7
From: Hansen, V
Subject: Re: Recent Developments

Charlotte,

The interview turned out as well as we had hoped. The witness corroborated the basic story of the other witnesses plus added some other details. She also described feeling as if something was wrong and that people were "covering up." She was with a family member in the triage area of the ED at the time of the incident. She was separated from the defendant and the victim by a curtain. I'm sure that the defense attorney (assuming the case goes to trial) will try to show that it was mistaken identity. But it looks like these two patients were the only ones in the ED at the time, other than an infant with a severe ear infection that had kept his parents awake that night.

Okay, you're on for coffee tomorrow at 11 AM!

Veronica

To: Stone, Charlotte P
Date: Monday, February 9
From: Strong, James Y
Subject: Re: Exams

Hi!

I've got my administrative assistant tracking down my itinerary for next week. I am looking forward to the summit, and the chance to get away, always a good thing now and then. Did I ever tell you that your VP for Research is a good friend of mine? I'm looking forward to reconnecting with him as well.

Do you have an area targeted for your dissertation, now that you've passed the qualifying exam? In some programs, students sometimes have their dissertations well under way by the time they take the exam, while others haven't even decided on a topic yet. Just wondering.

All the best

Jim

James Y Strong, PhD
Dean, School of Science
South Central State

To: Strong, James Y
Date: Monday, February 9
From: Stone, Charlotte P
Subject: Re: Exams

Hello,

Well, funny you should mention the dissertation topic. I did have a topic, and some data collected, but circumstances that have nothing to do with me have resulted in the possibility of dropping that idea and trying to come up with something else. So, I'm giving myself permission to think about it for a week or so.

When you find your schedule, maybe we can decide a time to meet.

Charlotte

To: Stone, Charlotte P
Date: Monday, February 9
From: Strong, James Y
Subject: Re: Exams

Well, I wouldn't let a change of dissertation focus worry you too much at your stage of the game. As a student, you are not always aware of all of the political forces involved in academia. Sometimes it is just easier to "cooperate and graduate."

All the best

Jim

James Y Strong, PhD
Dean, School of Science
South Central State

To: Strong, James Y
Date: Monday, February 9
From: Stone, Charlotte P
Subject: Re: Exams

Thanks. I'll keep that in mind. I'm trying not to take the situation personally. CS

To: Hansen, V
Date: Monday, February 9
From: Stone, Charlotte P
Subject: Monday AM

Hi Veronica,

Well, here it is barely past 9AM, and I've already had a couple of emails from Dr. Strong. I'm still not sure exactly when he's arriving.

I had fun at coffee yesterday. The mercy killing case sounds very interesting. You could definitely write a book about it when you're done. But, of course, some of the story has yet to be written. I guess it will depend, in part, on whether or not the DA decides to prosecute. If that happens, will the family drop its wrongful death case? Or will they pursue it anyway?

Lauren is on a field trip today. I had to get her to school by 6AM! They were going on an architectural tour of Columbus, then over to Brown County for a hike before returning. I need to pick her up at the school at 4:30. She was excited about it. Evidently, they are studying "what makes a community" in social studies and their text points out Columbus as an example.

I need to get to work. I hope that your day is going well.

Charlotte

To: Stone, Charlotte P
Date: Monday, February 9
From: Hansen, V
Subject: Monday PM

Hi there Charlotte,

My workday went okay. Now I'm looking forward to a quick and simple dinner in my PJs and two hours of my favorite TV shows! It is my reward for putting up with my finicky coworkers, even though today went pretty smoothly.

Before I forget, what did Pete have to say about the "banishment" or the possible change of dissertation topic (if anything) when he dropped Lauren off last night? I'm just curious about that. Also, do you think that the two of you will do anything for Valentine's Day? Has he mentioned it at all?

I had fun yesterday, too. You are correct, our lives are never dull, especially right now. Are there people alive who are truly bored? They must lack the ability to look around them!

Well, time for my first show to start. Have a good evening.

Veronica

To: Hansen, V
Date: Tuesday, February 10
From: Stone, Charlotte P
Subject: Re: Monday PM

Hi Veronica,

I had a nice quiet evening last night. Lauren came home exhausted from her little trip. She didn't have any homework, so we stopped at the grocery and picked out what my Mom used to call TV dinners (Lauren loves to do this) and ate them in front of the TV on a school night. That was our big treat!

As far as Pete goes, he said very little about the banishment and dissertation topic. He just asked if I had heard anything beyond the meeting ban, and I told him no, I was still waiting. That was about it. As far as Valentine's Day…no mention whatsoever. I don't know what to expect, if anything. He continues to be cordial, even helpful. But he hasn't initiated any social contact since my birthday. As I've said, I've wondered if he is dating. But I don't have any evidence to support that idea. And I really don't feel up to asking him. I just can't deal with that right now. So, I've chosen to maintain our status quo for the moment.

Here's what has me upset at this point in time: I got another one of those nasty emails this AM. Actually, the time of arrival was 2:37 AM. More sexual nastiness, this one calls me an "HIVho." That's who it is addressed To: "Dear HIVho." The message is only one word: "slaughter."

What kind of a crazy, sick person is doing this? And why are they targeting me? I think I will report this to our university IT people since these emails don't show any signs of stopping. I really don't think that Max, Pete, or anyone that knows me at SomaRx would do something like this, but I don't know anyone else who would, either. And the timing, coming at the same time as the "banishment," makes me wonder.

OK, well I need to get ready for a meeting. Have a good day.

Charlotte

To: Stone, Charlotte P
Date: Tuesday, February 10
From: Hansen, V
Subject: Concern

Hi Charlotte,

I hope that by the time you read this, you have reported the latest nasty emails to the university IT department. Spam is one thing – but what you're receiving sounds like an entirely different ball game. I'm a little worried, especially because of the "banishment." The two things (email and the banishment) may be unrelated, but they fact that they occurred at about the same time worries me a little, too. Actually, more than a little.

I am furiously working on getting all of the reports related to the mercy killing case finished, proofread, and organized with a table of contents into a coherent package. This will be given to the district attorney in the county where the incident took place. He will then decide whether or not to file charges in the matter. I would bet that charges will be filed. We'll see.

Take care of yourself, please!! Call if you need anything – I mean that!

Veronica

To: Hansen, V
Date: Wednesday, February 11
From: Stone, Charlotte P
Subject: Weird occurrences squared

Hi Veronica,

Well, here's the first weird occurrence. Jake (remember him?) called me last night to intercede for Max. "Listen, I'm not sure of the details of what happened, but I do know that Max is really, really sorry and entirely broken up over it." (Can you believe that?) "He really wishes that you would at least talk to him about it." (Why do I feel like I'm back in junior high?)

I told Jake that it sounded like he was a good friend. I needed some more "cooling off" time, but Max could call me in a week or two and we could talk. (I didn't know what else to say. I didn't want to give Jake any of the details that he doesn't already know.) Besides, I can either talk to Max or not, depending on how I feel later. I DO need more time...that's for sure. And I don't want to deal with Max until Valentine's Day is in the past.

Second occurrence: the "email of the day" in my university account. This one isn't quite so bad. It is to "Cherie" from "your friend from France" and the attachment (which contains a virus, I'm sure) is entitled "your naughty pictures." Hmm.

I hope that your final report is shaping up well. Maybe you have finished it. Do you think that the MD involved has any clue that potential charges are a possibility for his future? Is he aware of the potential for the civil suit?

I am being careful. I don't feel threatened in any way, except by these emails; which, as you have pointed out, are most likely the work of a coward. I will call you if I need anything, believe me.

Take care,

Charlotte

To: Stone, Charlotte P
Date: Thursday, February 12
From: Strong, James Y
Subject: Re: Exams

Hi!

I found out that I will be arriving at your airport around 1:15 PM on Tuesday, February 24. I will be renting a car. How about if I call you when I arrive? I'll meet you somewhere for a quick bite to eat.

All the best

Jim

James Y Strong, PhD
Dean, School of Science
South Central State

To: Strong, James Y
Date: Thursday, February 12
From: Stone, Charlotte P
Subject: Re: Exam

Early afternoon sounds fine. I don't have any classes or meetings at that time, and I have flexibility in my work schedule. In case you don't already have it, my office phone is 555-0047. Will look forward to seeing you then. CS

To: Stone, Charlotte P
Date: Thursday, February 12
From: Hansen, V
Subject: Valentine's Week

Hi Charlotte,

Yeah, the entire Valentines' thing must be a little awkward for you. (By the way, I think you are very wise to postpone any encounters with Max until after Feb. 14, if at all.) I've been struggling with what to give to Van. He hasn't asked me what I want. For some reason, I'm afraid that he is going to give me a ring, maybe even an engagement ring. The funny thing is, we've discussed our feelings about marriage at our age, and we're both against it, in principle, anyway. But, you know what? If he would ask me, I think I would do it! Maybe this fear of the gift, is actually my projection of my own fear that I would do something I said I would never do (get married again.) So, I'm trying to work out how I would hand it if Van "pops the question." Part of it would hinge on how he asked me! I just don't know. I guess I'll just wait and see what happens. Watch- he'll give me an automatic can opener or something. (Last year he gave me a freezer for my birthday! Before you jump to conclusions, I did ask for one.)

I guess I will hope and pray that I will handle the gifting situation with grace and courtesy, no matter what he gives me, assuming that he gives me something. I got him a bed and breakfast gift certificate to a B&B that has the reputation of being haunted, but different from the place we went over New Year's. I also got him a Valentine card that is just perfect, because it has a punch line that reflects an inside joke related to a client we both worked with.

This is your weekend with Lauren, right? Maybe you could take a valentine over from Lauren, and have your own available if he gives you one. If not, it stays hidden. Just one way you could handle it.

I'm meeting Van for a drink in a little bit. The district attorney was supposed to call him today – maybe charges have been filed against the mercy killer already.

Take care.

Veronica

To: Hansen, V
Date: Thursday, February 12
From: Stone, Charlotte P
Subject: Re: Valentine's Week

Hi Veronica,

I am convinced that great minds think alike. I had already purchased red paper, lace, glue and glitter so that Lauren could make a card for her dad. We'll do that tomorrow night. I'll make a small one after Lauren goes to sleep. I also got a collection of Pete's favorite chocolates from the chocolatier on the Circle downtown including nonpareils and chocolate-covered almonds. I also got a few of those conversation hearts with funny sayings on them. So, I'm prepared. We'll go over to Pete's on Sunday, and if he gives me something, I've got my gift ready.

I'm exhausted. I think I am feeling the stress, waiting to hear about the official data elimination, or something. I have my library novel. I think I'll get to bed early, read a little, and try to get eight hours' worth of sleep for a change.

Have a good evening.

Charlotte

To: Stone, Charlotte P
Date: Friday, February 13
From: Stone, Peter E
Subject: Question

Hi Charlotte,

Can I stop by the apartment this afternoon at about 5 (after work)? I have something that I want to drop off.

Pete

To: Stone, Peter E
Date: Friday, February 13
From: Stone, Charlotte P
Subject: Re: Question

Hi Pete,

Sure – I should be home by then.

Charlotte

To: Stone, Charlotte P
Date: Friday, February 13
From: Hansen, V
Subject: Re: Valentine's Week

Hi Charlotte,

Yes, I do think that great minds think alike. I've decided to just chill and not worry any more about the "big question." I'm just going to enjoy the weekend, come what may.

Besides, I've got plenty of other stuff to think about. Charges have been filed against the mercy killer. I guess he didn't see it coming at all. Bail has yet to be set. Very interesting. Watch tomorrow morning's paper for sure – as well as the evening news on TV. Van may even get his nose in the picture; he's been around the county courthouse all day.

How is your email situation coming? I'm assuming there haven't been any more nasty messages?

Veronica

To: Hansen, V
Date: Friday, February 13
From: Stone, Charlotte P
Subject: Re: Valentine's Week

Hi Veronica,

Well, the emails are still coming, sometimes two in one day. All are nasty and insulting. I just delete them as they come in. They stay in a "deleted" folder. Our IT detective will come and examine them once a week and do any follow-up necessary. Of course, if there are any direct threats, I'm to contact him immediately. He says that this type of thing usually comes to an end in a week or two. A couple of other people, both faculty members, have been targeted in similar ways in the last few years. He says I'm the first student that he's encountered receiving this particular type of email at the School of Nursing. I'm trying not to dwell on it. He also installed a spyware program on my computer and ran it. It found a couple of things, but nothing really bad. We did find one cookie, "teaser," that I can't figure out. It is connected to a website that features brain teasers, jokes, etc. I know that I've never gone to it.

Pete is coming over tonight for a while! Today (the 12th) is actually the anniversary of our engagement. I wonder if he is bringing a gift? If so, I'm really not prepared, but I don't have time to worry about it now. I'll keep you posted.

Charlotte

To: Stone, Charlotte P
Date: Friday, February 13
From: Hansen, V
Subject: Re: Valentine's Week

Charlotte,

Well, that IS interesting, that Pete is dropping by on a personal anniversary. Let me know how it turns out.

I'm going to watch the local news. Van just called. Things are happening! He is still at the courthouse. I'm sure this will be a field day for the press! I'll write more later.

Veronica

To: Hansen, V
Date: Friday, February 13
From: Stone, Charlotte P
Subject: Re: Valentine's Week

Hi Veronica,

Well, Pete stopped by to deliver another bud vase. This one was made of copper and held an American Beauty rose. There was no card. I thanked him. He refused coffee or a beer, and only stayed a few minutes. I thought the whole thing was rather strange. He never mentioned our engagement anniversary, either.

I saw the story about the mercy killer MD twice last night; once on the 10 o'clock news (Channel 8) and once on the 11 o'clock news (Channel 13). You were right, the press is having a field day. It must be exciting for you, to have been involved in this from an early stage.

I'm going to do some cleaning, then take Lauren for a walk, then read my book for a while. Have a good weekend.

Charlotte

To: Stone, Charlotte P
Date: Friday, February 13
From: Oberon
Subject: My sweet

My Titania:

I dream of you, and our dreams connect.

I am your one, your only, true love. Sleep well, my sweet. Soon I will possess you totally.

Oberon

XXXXX

To: Stone, Charlotte P
Date: Saturday, February 14
From: Hansen, V
Subject: New question

Hi Charlotte,

You're right about the mercy killer. It is exciting to see this work come to some sort of fruition.

I've just thought of a bothersome question. How do you know that Dr. Strong is who he says he is? Maybe he is some kind of lunatic that is masquerading to be Dr. Strong. Maybe he's the one sending the nasty emails!

Veronica

To: Hansen, V
Date: Saturday, February 14
From: Stone, Charlotte P
Subject: New question

Hi Veronica,

Our university IT guy was ahead of you. He checked into the source of the Dr. Strong emails and said that they were legit. The nasty ones are coming from two different place, and those return addresses may be forged, anyway. He also found a picture of Dr. Strong, so I will know what he looks like. But, everything seems A-OK on that front. You can never be too careful. The IT guy is also going to check with SomaRx's IT guy. He thinks that angle (a SomaRx connection) is the most likely.

Thanks for being concerned. How does Van feel right now (and you, too)? Victorious?!

I would think you both deserve a pat on the back for a job well done! Or maybe champagne!

Charlotte

To: Stone, Charlotte P
Date: Saturday, February 14
From: Hansen, V
Subject: Valentine Victory?

Hi Charlotte,

Thanks for your congratulations. Yes, we were feeling pretty victorious – still are as a matter of fact. We did go out and bought a bottle of champagne, then put it on ice. This time, Van took me for a carriage ride, and then to the Canterbury where a finely appointed room awaited! We ordered in...room service. The food was almost as good as the French cuisine we'd had previously. It was a wonderful, romantic night. He liked my gift. And he gave me a ring, but it really wasn't an engagement ring. It was a peridot that had belonged to his grandmother. He had it put in a modern ring setting with two small diamonds flanking it. It had been a pendant. He said his grandmother wore it frequently because it had been the first gift of jewelry she had received from his grandfather. Peridot was her birthstone. I love it. I think it is the perfect gift. I feel honored that he would give me a family heirloom; that means a lot to me. Van says he never thought about giving it to anyone else...but giving it to me "feels right."

Ahem! Enough on that topic. How has your weekend been going?

Take care – Veronica

To: Hansen, V
Date: Saturday, February 14
From: Stone, Charlotte P
Subject: Valentine Entropy?

Hi Veronica,

That subject line doesn't make sense, but I couldn't think of anything else. Lauren and I went over to Pete's and took our valentines. We called first. Pete was cordial enough and had coffee for us and hot chocolate for Lauren. Lauren gave him her valentine, and then went to play with the toys that she keeps over there. I gave Pete mine, he smiled when he read it and put it on the mantel with Lauren's. He didn't have one for me, but I suppose the bud vase was my valentine, like my engagement ring was on February 12th, 12 years ago. We sat and chatted pleasantly for about a half hour. Then Lauren and I left because she had choir practice. So that was it...just kind of ordinary. If we were still living together, it would seem fairly normal (except I would expect Pete to kiss me under those circumstances). But there was no kiss, or even a hug. This is weird. What are we to each other...Pete and I? We're not really ex-spouses. We're not really spouses. When I feel a little less fragile, I need to have a discussion with him...or maybe even suggest counseling. But right now, I just feel like I can't deal with it. When the questions regarding the data are answered and my dissertation is on somewhat on track again, maybe I'll feel ready to tackle those issues.

I received another email from "Oberon"...creepy, but predictable. I'm not worrying about that, I need to deal with my real problems.

Well, continue to bask in your glory as long as you can. You deserve it!

Congratulations again,

Charlotte

To: Stone, Charlotte P
Date: Sunday, February 15
From: Hansen, V
Subject: Re: Valentine Entropy?

Hi Charlotte,

I hope you are not feeling too "down." I agree, the relationship between you and Pete sounds a little strange, and maybe strained, too. I also understand your need to just "let it be" for a week or two before confronting your need for more direction and definition. Hang in there. Things will get better soon. And it is never too late, or too early, for counseling. I hope it doesn't sound like I am harping on that topic, I just know that I have found it extremely helpful in my own life.

As far as the dissertation, I also feel like that will work out, with time. It is kind of strange that you are the first to notice something unusual with the trends in the numbers. But you are the first one that is heading toward any kind of report regarding it, so maybe your discovery really isn't that unusual. Anyhow, at this point, you have done all that you can – so you just need to wait now, probably the most difficult part.

I will get the chance to observe a lot of the trial process regarding the mercy killer. I wonder what will happen regarding his license, since it was already suspended once and he served his "sentence" that the Board of Medicine handed down. Of course, if he stays in jail...he won't be practicing there! This will be a great opportunity for me, I'll get to observe the process from beginning to end. The arraignment is tomorrow.

Veronica

To: Hansen, V
Date: Monday, February 16
From: Stone, Charlotte P
Subject: Maybe you're right

Hi Veronica,

Maybe you're right about the counseling. Do you have someone that you'd recommend?

It just hit me that I am still on Pete's health insurance (after all, we ARE still married!) and we have a cafeteria plan benefit for treatment not covered by the general policy. I'm sure that counseling would fall in this category, and worrying about the cost is NOT a reason to put it off. I think I'll try it. Actually, I was in counseling years ago, and I did find it very helpful. In fact, after the crisis that brought me to counseling in the first place was resolved, I kept going for a year longer, just because I found it so beneficial in my day-to-day life. However, I found out about eight months after terminating with that counselor that she had died of cancer. I had no idea that she had been ill, and I felt very sad about her passing.

Here I was telling my counselor all of my problems, and she was dying, which was much worse than anything that I was dealing with. I will need a referral if I am to go into therapy again, since returning to my previous therapist is not an option.

I am going to try and take your advice about just letting my dissertation "be" for a while. I'll give myself a week off from worrying about it. It will feel strange to miss the research meeting this week, though. I've been going for almost a year.

Your life sounds like it will get even more exciting. You'd better take notes – I'm sure that you could write a best seller about this case!

Take care – Charlotte

To: Stone, Charlotte P
Date: Monday, February 16
From: Hansen, V
Subject: Re: Maybe you're right

Hi Charlotte,

I would recommend Ray Morrison. His office happens to be fairly close to where you live. But I would recommend him, even if you lived a hundred miles away! I went to him for seven years, he really helped me sort out my relationship issues. He practices with his wife, that is, they own the business together, but they are never there at the same time. I think they actually have two offices; one on the north side, and one on the south. I think they alternate going to the different offices.

Work is dragging today, which is highly unusual. But, the gossip mill is very active! It sounds like the MDs are unhappy, and there may be a split in one of the bigger psychiatry groups that admits patients to this hospital.

Oh well...back to work!

Veronica

To: Hansen, V
Date: Monday, February 16
From: Stone, Charlotte P
Subject: Did it!

Hi Veronica,

Well, I looked up the number for Ray Morrison's practice and called and left a message. He returned my call about an hour later. He sounds so kind and so gentle and so polite, but direct! We'll see how this goes. I agree that counseling could be very beneficial for me and

I've had a very positive experience before. My previous counselor was female. I think this could be a very different type of experience. Men think so differently! But...nothing ventured, nothing gained! I'm willing to give it a try. I have an appointment a week from today.

On my lunch hour, I walked over to the union building and bought a new notebook with a bright pink cover. If I had more funds available, I would have gone for one of those fabric covered journals, but the pink notebook will do the job. I'm going to try and start to journal again. I found that very helpful during my last counseling experience. And I do actually like to sit and write with pencil on paper. The day was bright and sunshiny and it was good to get outside, so that was another added benefit. I'm becoming more optimistic. Maybe I'll be able to make some sense out of the crazy thing that my life has become. After I picked up Lauren, we walked over to the Starbucks near our apartment. I got some coffee and I bought Lauren a hot chocolate. She started on her homework and I started on my journal. We were there about a half hour. I can't afford Starbucks on a daily basis, but it was a nice little treat. We came home and Lauren watched an after school special on TV while I started some laundry that has been piling up. Later on, we watched "Jeopardy" together. Even though Lauren knows very few of the answers (or should I say, questions?) she really enjoys this show. She keeps on the edge of her seat, waiting for the few questions that she really knows the answers to, (or vice versa). Well, all in all – I'm feeling calmer and more optimistic. Thank you for the counselor referral. I think it was an excellent suggestion.

I hope that your day ended on a positive note.

Charlotte

To: Stone, Charlotte P
Date: Monday, February 16
From: Hansen, V
Subject: Good for you!

Hi Charlotte,

I'm so glad that you have decided to try counseling. I knew that Ray would call you back within an hour or two. He is by far the most considerate, insightful, and unselfish man that I have ever met. It sounds like you have glimpsed some of those qualities by your brief telephone conversation with him. Yes, I don't doubt that a counseling experience with a man will be different from a counseling experience with a woman. But, you are going into the experience with that insight, so you won't be "blindsided" by the difference, like some people might be.

Yesterday's work pace continued to be slow throughout the day. Like I've said, slowness is very unusual at our unit, and especially so for a Monday. I wonder if it is related to the MD conflict. Possibly, they are postponing admissions until all of that is settled (?). I think that hypothesis could be close to the truth. We all have our ears perked up at work. Something is bound to happen within the next few days. You may have seen the in the paper that Dr. van Reedy's (I feel I can name him now, since the charges are public) arraignment is set for tomorrow. I'd love to be there, and maybe if the slow pace continues at work, I can arrange that. But I can't count on it. (Darn!) Anyhow, once the date has been set for the trial, I will arrange some vacation around it. I want to see as much of the courtroom process as possible. Due to my "second job" with Van, I'll get to see a lot of the paperwork beforehand.

Lauren is a very smart little girl. And she is making herself even smarter by watching a show like Jeopardy. A lot of seven-year-olds wouldn't have the patience to sit through a show where they didn't know many of the answers!

Keep up with the journal. I think it is a great idea!

Veronica

To: Hansen, V
Date: Tuesday, February 17
From: Stone, Charlotte P
Subject: Messages from the Subconscious

Hi Veronica,

I'm warning you – I'm in kind of a giddy mood. I don't know why. I woke up about a half hour earlier than usual. It may have something to do with the journaling. I had a lot of dreams last night, and I remember a few of them. I may start keeping my journal next to my bed so it will be handy if I want to write one down in the middle of the night, or first thing in the morning.

Anyhow – I think one of the dreams is pretty funny. Here is how it went:

First I am my "self" of twenty years ago. My hair looks like it did in my undergraduate days. I'm barefoot and wearing jeans and a tie-dye T shirt. I see this cute boy. He looks pretty generic, like no one I know (or ever knew). I have this vague sense that he was blond. In other words, he's kind of a generic pretty boy. I feel attracted to him, so I think: "I will have sex with him. There is no reason why not. I am not married. I just need to keep it safe." So I locate a condom somewhere.

The scene shifts, and I am in the back seat of a car. Someone else is driving, but I have no idea who it is, I didn't "see" this person, the driver. The mood is anticipatory, like maybe I'm on my way to meet the blond guy. It is bright summertime, but probably evening.

Anyhow, I look to my left and there is this old lady sitting next to me. I'm horrified – this ruins everything!!!! All of a sudden, the car takes off way too fast down a hill and crashes at the bottom, where the road ends in a T intersection.

Even as I write this, I'm laughing. Katy (my former counselor) took a very Gestalt view of many dreams, and I would agree with that philosophy on this one. Meaning, I am the young person, the old lady, maybe even the unseen driver of the car. It's a pretty clear depiction about how I feel about my life right now! Ray will have his work cut out for him!

Hope your day goes well. I'm on my way to the office.

Charlotte

To: Stone, Charlotte P
Date: Tuesday, February 17
From: Hansen, V
Subject: Re: Messages from the Subconscious

Hi Charlotte,

I loved the account of your dream! And yes, the interpretation seems obvious. You are between youth and old age. You are trying to sort out your direction, and things appear to be going downhill really fast! But, at the bottom of the hill, you really have two choices (at least!) Yes, Ray will have his work cut out for him, but he will probably enjoy having a client who has the amount of insight that you do.

Robyn and I went for a grandmother/granddaughter after-school outing today. We went to the bookstore and I got another mystery for her. I told her that every time she finishes a book, I will buy her another one. She is averaging about a book a week. I got a book about the 1800s in Hawaii. (Did you know that there were leper colonies there?) You just never know what you will find at a bookstore! Always something interesting. Sometimes I feel pessimistic about where our society is headed, but when I go to a bookstore, my faith is restored!

Afterwards, we drove a few blocks from the bookstore to a cute little sandwich shop where they also have great pies (all homemade – as is their sandwich bread.) We each had a cinnamon roll. Robyn had milk and I had coffee. Robyn told me this funny little story. I guess she has been technically "naughty," but I can't blame her for it... she has a friend whose mother is engaged, and the mom and her fiance are looking for a new house. So, Robyn's friend's house has just been put on the market, and there is one of those little brochure holders on their front lawn. Robyn doesn't want this friend to move, so she stole all of the brochures. The friend's mom just thinks that a lot of people are REALLY interested in the house. I'm trying to stay neutral, at least when I'm talking to Robyn. I asked her if she thought that disappearing brochures would keep her friend's house from selling, and all she would say is "it shouldn't hurt." I feel better knowing that the friend will most likely stay in the school district, so the move shouldn't mean that they won't see each other again.

OK – I'm dozing off at the computer – time to close this and get to bed.

Veronica

To: Hansen, V
Date: Wednesday, February 18
From: Stone, Charlotte P
Subject: Surprise

Hi Veronica,

I hope that you got a good night's sleep last night and that your Wednesday at work went well. I had a strange surprise during my lunch hour. Actually, it was about 11:45 and I was trying to tie up a few loose ends before leaving my desk in the research office. I was just about ready to log off of my computer when I could hear someone asking where my desk was. Then, Max walked into my cubicle, wearing scrubs and a lab coat. He looked like he came across the courtyard from the hospital.

I must have looked shocked (because I was, sort of). He looked kind of stern, or serious. He said, "Look, I know I behaved badly a few weeks ago. I was wrong, and I am truly sorry. I want to see you again, when and if you feel ready. I waited for you before and I'll wait for you again. The ball is in your court. We can see each other only in broad daylight on campus if that is the way you want it. I just want you to know that I am truly sorry." Then he left one of his business cards on the corner of my desk and was gone.

I was speechless then. I'm still kind of "mentally speechless," meaning I don't know what to do next. Any advice? Men are such a mystery to me! I guess I don't know how to handle this type of apology. He did sound sincere. Maybe I'll just email him (now that I have his email address) and let him know that I accept his apology, and leave it at that for now(?). I really do need some help with this – I'm out of my comfort zone. Any advice will be appreciated!

Thanks in advance.

Charlotte

To: Stone, Charlotte P
Date: Wednesday, February 18
From: Hansen, V
Subject: Re: Surprise

Hi Charlotte,

Well, a man who apologizes. And with witnesses (assuming that someone outside your cubicle was listening in – a pretty safe bet). Well...I don't have a lot of experience with that sort of thing (male apologies, that is.) It's really pretty gutsy, and I mean that in a good way. But, I'm still suspicious of him.

Your appointment with Ray can't come too soon! You've got a lot going on!

Dr. van Reedy is out on bail. Pretty hard to argue that one, because it has been years since the alleged crime without any other blots on his record. He served the "sentence" of the state Board of Medicine without any problem AND did hours of community service that were required. He continues to donate 5 to 10 hour per week to a community shelter. It is hard to justify keeping someone in jail with that kind of record.

Now it is my turn to ask the questions: What are you going to do about Max?? I think your life is becoming pretty interesting, even complicated. Any more developments in the matter of SomaRx?

Let me know if you need anything.

Veronica

To: Hansen, V
Date: Thursday, February 19
From: Stone, Charlotte P
Subject: Re: Surprise

Hi Veronica,

Well, I've slept on it...the issue of Max, that is. He's probably an okay guy. He's probably having second thoughts about the wedding night. Wow, that sounds strange, maybe even Freudian! I guess I should say: the night of the wedding. Maybe I'll send him an email today, simply stating that I accept his apology. But I will also tell him that life is too uncertain right now for any form of dating. I have some personal and professional issues to sort out first.

Although Max is not a "front runner" in my list of "suspects" regarding the nasty emails, I still wonder if he is behind it. I don't really think so, but he has that "dark side" that I got a glimpse of that night a few weeks ago. Maybe that "dark side" extends further and deeper. Maybe he has too much time on his hands, and too much hatred toward women. I doubt it though, as a pediatrician, he has to communicate with the moms of the babies all the time. Still, maybe some times he gets very, very sick of that style of communication.

All right...I'm probably ruminating on this too much. Probably because it distracts me from my real issue, which is the data, the dissertation, the "banishment." To answer your question about SomaRx, I won't be going to any research meetings until I get the word from Dr. Mueller about my project. Obviously, if I can't finish my dissertation topic, I won't be going back at all. Until this matter is settled ... I just feel like I can't really deal with anything else. Behind this "in limbo" feeling, is a strong "bad girl" feeling- like I've done something wrong, like I've been caught with my hand in the cookie jar. I keep repeating to myself: "I haven't done anything wrong. I haven't done anything wrong." I feel like it is some kind of mantra. But as often as I repeat it I still don't believe it. I can't shake the "bad girl" feeling. I think that I really need to see Ray.

Charlotte

To: Stone, Charlotte P
Date: Thursday, February 19
From: Hansen, V
Subject: Re: Surprise

Hi Charlotte,

Well, if it makes you feel any better, you didn't do anything wrong! But, it's no wonder that you feel that way. There is so much secrecy involved with whatever is going on. And – you are being punished for something, and you are not even sure what it is that you did to "deserve" it.

This has been a rather ordinary day for me (if there is such a thing). I had a couple of inpatient admissions, but I didn't feel rushed, so the pace was comfortable. All of the people being admitted were pretty straightforward. That's kind of unusual, at least two-thirds of those I admit seem to have some sort of agenda, which means the admission takes more time.

Did you email Max? Any response? I do have some admiration for him due to his apology, I admit it!

Isn't your oral defense tomorrow? Are you nervous?

Hang in there. My thoughts are with you.

Veronica

To: Hansen, V
Date: Friday, February 20
From: Stone, Charlotte P
Subject: It is today

Hi Veronica,

I'm up early today. I woke up at 4:45 and couldn't get back to sleep.

Thanks for your "good thoughts." Yes, my oral defense is today. I'm not super worried about it. I reviewed my notes that I wrote down after the written exam and jotted down a few more regarding the things that I wish that I had done differently. I think that is really all I need to do. I'm not nervous about this oral defense at all.

As far as Max goes...yes, I emailed yesterday from my university email account (I don't want him to know my personal email address at this time.) Yes – I have to say that I admire him for apologizing, too. I'm just not ready for personal relationships yet, if ever. I told him that I accepted his apology, but I wasn't ready for dating three weeks ago...or now. I have a lot of professional and personal concerns on my plate and maybe when these are resolved, I'll reconsider. As of yesterday at 3:30 PM, I did not have an answer from him.

OK, I need to hit the shower, get Lauren's breakfast and get on with my day. Hope yours is a good one!

Charlotte

To: Stone, Charlotte P
Date: Friday, February 19
From: Stone, Peter E
Subject: Missed you

Charlotte,

I missed you at the research meeting yesterday. I'm taking it that things are still up in the air re: your dissertation topic. I'll pick up Lauren between 5 and 5:30 this afternoon, if that is okay.

Pete

To: Hansen, V
Date: Friday, February 20
From: Stone, Charlotte
Subject: Crash

Veronica,

It is me again. I came home a little early, too upset and emotionally worn out to do anything productive. The lack of sleep last night probably didn't help.

My oral defense of the qualifying exam went fine. It was actually pretty short. The dean, who is on my committee, was very complimentary about the written exam. She said that I'm a good writer and scientist. She said that I should trust her, because she's been around a long time, and has read a lot of qualifying exams. The members of the committee had a few questions, I answered them, then I was asked to leave the room. When they asked me to com back in they told me that I had passed (which is what I had expected).

About an hour later, Dr. Fleming stopped by. She complimented me on my exam (she's the chairperson of my committee, and was there of course, during the defense). Then, she said that Dr. Mueller of SomaRx had asked that I remove myself from the antidepressant project. This means that I will never go to meetings again.

Furthermore, all of the data that I now have must be "destroyed." I'll turn in the disks that I have. Also the deletion of the data from my files, both at my office and at home, must be carried out by SomaRx's biostatistics department.

So...two big events, neither one a big surprise, but still, I feel exhausted and overwhelmed. But right now, I have to get Lauren from school and get her ready to go with Pete this evening.

Take care.

Charlotte

To: Stone, Charlotte P
Date: Friday, February 20
From: Hansen, V
Subject: Re: Crash

Hey Charlotte,

I feel badly for you! My hunch is that you probably suspected the ending of your involvement with the SomaRx project. Do you think that Dr. Fleming delayed telling you until after your oral defense?

At least now you know where you stand. And maybe you can move forward with your life. After you think about it, you can probably salvage some of your previous work on your dissertation and apply it elsewhere.

Be good to yourself this weekend. I'll be getting together with Van in the evenings but how about getting together for Sunday brunch? Also call me if you need to talk tomorrow AM. (Or in an emergency, you can call my cell anytime.)

Take care –

Veronica

To: Hansen, V
Date: Saturday, February 21
From: Hansen, V
Subject: Re: Crash

Hi Veronica,

Well, I'm up early again. My counseling session with Ray can't come soon enough.

In answer to your question, yes, I do think that Dr. Fleming had held "the verdict" for a while and delayed telling me about the permanence of the "banishment" until the oral defense was over. I feel a little angry about that; but I have to admit, the delay probably helped me to concentrate better on my defense.

I just can't shake the feeling of having my hand slapped. As ridiculous as it is, I still can't get rid of the feeling of being a guilty party...but to what?? I think that I will do some heavy-duty cleaning around here, together with the laundry and some long walks, anything to keep moving, keep busy and not think about anything else. I just got my hair cut a few weeks ago ... so that is out as a coping strategy. I have a key to the research office. As a last resort, maybe I'll go in there and do some filing. But, on the other hand, that may not be such a good idea. Maybe I'll go to a movie, even though I don't usually like to go alone.

I mentioned my "news" to Pete last night when he came over. He was sympathetic. But we didn't talk about it much, mostly because I didn't want to, especially in front of Lauren.

Well, it is light out now. I think I'll go for a walk. I may call you later.

Charlotte

PS – thanks for the brunch invitation, but I'm kind of strapped financially, and I'm in such a down mood anyway. How about if we meet for coffee at 11 at the usual Sunday spot? Even though I feel like holing up for the weekend, I'm going to force myself to get out and do a few things, including going to church on Sunday.

To: Stone, Charlotte P
Date: Saturday, February 21
From: Hansen, V
Subject: Re: Crash

Hi Charlotte,

Of course, we can meet at the usual spot. I'll be looking forward to it. I'm also glad that you've made a to-do list, and will be staying active. It sounds like you want the weekend to go by quickly. Just remember to pamper yourself a little along the way. As far as going to movies alone...I've done it for years. Once I found my seat in the theater the first time, I was fine! Now, I really enjoy going alone. Which is a good thing, because Van really doesn't enjoy going to a theater at all.

I'll see you tomorrow. Remember, call if you need anything!

Veronica

To: Stone, Charlotte P
Date: Saturday, February 21
From: Stone, Peter E
Subject: Tomorrow evening

Hey Charlotte,

I just tried to call the apartment, but you must be out. How about coming over here for dinner tomorrow around 5? I'm sure Mom will fix something good. Then you can take Lauren home after that, when you're ready.

Pete

To: Stone, Peter E
Date: Saturday, February 21
From: Stone, Charlotte P
Subject: Tomorrow evening

Hello Pete,

Yes, I'd like that. I'll be there.

Charlotte

To: Hansen, V
Date: Saturday, February 21
From: Stone, Charlotte P
Subject: Re:Crash

Hi Veronica,

OK, I will see you tomorrow. Have a good time tonight with Van.

Pete just emailed me. He's invited me to supper at his parents' place tomorrow. For some reason, that makes me feel better. After that, I'll be bringing Lauren home with me, and I won't be in this apartment by myself.

Till tomorrow,

Charlotte

To: Hansen, V
Date: Monday, February 23
From: Stone, Charlotte P
Subject: A new week

Hi Veronica,

Well, once again, I'm up early. But I feel a little better. My appointment with Ray is at 2PM – thank goodness. I hope I just don't explode when I walk into his office with "Please help me!" or worse – like bursting into tears in the first five minutes. We're having some kind of group picture taken today – "we" being the doctoral students...so I need to dress up a little bit. I'll wear my navy blue suit, which I feel good in, in one way. I think navy is a good color for me, but sometimes I think that it makes me look like a nun. Whatever the case, it means that I'll be going to this appointment dressed a little more formally than I would like.

Thanks again for meeting me for a chat in person. I felt much better after that. The dinner at Pete's parents was okay. The food was good, of course, but I felt like the conversation was too cheerful. I think they were trying a little too hard to make me feel better. Maybe Pete felt even a little guilty. After I had Lauren situated in the car and walked around the back, Pete gave me a little squeeze and said that everything will turn out all right. No kiss. I said, "I don't know, I'm going for counseling, starting tomorrow." He looked a little surprised but didn't say anything more, and neither did I. The issue of his possible interest in someone else is still lurking in my mind, but I still can't address it with him. If he told me that he was seeing another person, I just don't think that I could handle it right now.

Well, time to try and beautify myself for the photo shoot. More later.

Charlotte

To: Stone, Charlotte P
Date: Monday, February 23
From: Hansen, V
Subject: Re: Chin up!

Hi Charlotte,

I don't have time to write a lot now, but keep your chin up! I know you will like Ray, and that he will be a "therapeutic ally."

I am sending good thoughts your way.

Veronica

To: Hansen, V
Date: Monday, February 23
From: Stone, Charlotte P
Subject: Re: The appointment

Hi Veronica,

Well, I think things went well at the appointment. Ray is a very nice guy. Like I thought, having a male counselor is extremely different from having a female counselor...at least from what I can tell right now. Of course, being the first session, a lot of the time was spent collecting information and laying down the ground rules. Then we got into the crux of the matter, as much as you can in a half hour or so. But I think Ray has the general idea of what I was working on. At one point, he asked me what I expected the future would hold. I had to answer, "I don't know – I guess that is why I am here." But I'd never really even thought of it that way. Maybe, with Ray as my ally, I can start to make plans and feel more in control.

At the end of the session, he said "I think that you are a person with a strong commitment to the truth." I said: "I don't have time to mess around." Game playing is not for me!

Anyhow – thank you, thank you, THANK YOU for the referral!! I do feel more optimistic now! And Dr. Strong arrives tomorrow, so at least, that will be somewhat of a distraction.

Charlotte

PS – I think that I forgot to tell you – but the SomaRx biostatisticians sent me an email at work. They want to arrange a time to get the data off my home computer by the end of this week. It sounds like the "data annihilation" is a priority.

To: Stone, Charlotte P
Date: Tuesday, February 24
From: Hansen, V
Subject: WARNING!! EXTREME CAUTION!

Charlotte,

Please, please be careful! I think you should cancel your meeting with JS. I don't care if he did fly in from Denver, or Timbuktu, for that matter. I have new information. I used some of the investigative websites that Van has access to (that he uses for his private investigator work.) I found out that James Y Strong IS the webmaster for the "Minerva's Voice" website at his university. So the fact that your name appears to be connected with it is no accident. I think there may be something sinister here. Also, Strong was abruptly removed from teaching responsibilities mid-semester a few years ago, which makes me wonder if he was transferred to an administration position because of something unsavory...like maybe he was "kicked upstairs" at his university. I've left a message on Van's cell phone, to see if he could find out if there is anything more in the criminal realm. No answer from him, so far.

But there's more. "Minerva's Voice" is not Strong's only website. He also has a general, goofy "joke" site. Most of the so-called jokes are either really stupid, insulting, or extremely childish. The insulting ones are directed at women. The stupid ones are generally toilet humor. Remember what Dr. Pierce at St. Joseph's said about the combination of fixations regarding women and bodily functions – not good!! Not the type of person you want to get involved with! Remember the cookie that you found on your computer called "teaser?" "Teaser" is part of this website belonging to Strong. He could be the one sending you all of the obscene email!

I'm going to leave a message on your cell and at your work. I hope you get one of these messages. Be careful. Call me as soon as you can.

Veronica

To: Hansen, V
Date: Tuesday, February 24
From: Stone, Charlotte P
Subject: Re: WARNING!! EXTREME CAUTION!

VERONICA!

I didn't receive either of your phone messages or email (until now). Everything is okay, I'm at home, just a little shaky. Pete is here...he took Lauren out of school a half-hour early. They're watching TV together. Or rather, Lauren is watching the TV, and Pete is staring at the screen. The police are coming by shortly to get statements from both of us.

Here's what happened:

Dr. Strong arrived in town and called my office from his cell. He arranged to pick me up in front of the library, which he did. He appeared pleasant; better looking than his picture would indicate. He was dressed casually, but very expensively, in a navy blazer, khakis, and blue button-down shirt. After the hellos, he said something like: "I know it is past your lunchtime, but I'm from a different time zone. Is there a place to eat close by that has good home-cooked food?" I suggested Schultz's because it is close, has a parking lot, and does have good home-cooked food.

So we drove over there, parked, and went in. He selected a pretty large meal. I got some coffee and dessert. By this time it was almost 2 PM, so were are only a few people in the place. We talked a lot about academics and research, and how it can be hard to get funding. He told me about some of the changes coming down the pike at his university. I told him some of the problems going on at the school of nursing. Really, there was no personal aspect to the conversation at all.

Then he started to ask me a few questions about the antidepressant that SomaRx is working on. I said, "Even though there aren't many people here right now, I'm not very comfortable discussing it here. Many people who eat here work at SomaRx. It's practically just across the street."

He took a sip of his coffee, then looked right at me, smiled and said: "Good. Let's head for a place a little more private." I felt slightly uncomfortable at this point. But, I told myself, his was a logical comment, given what I just said.

We went to his rental car. He opened the passenger door for me. I got a glimpse of a satchel with a zippered top on the back seat. The zipper wasn't completely closed. There was a gap of about three inches. I saw a half circle of silver-colored metal.

Three images floated into my mind almost instantaneously: First – do you remember about five years ago when a male (and married) graduate student killed a female student in his class and her sister? When the authorities caught him, he was openly sobbing, and that picture was on the front page of the newspaper. The motive was professional jealously. The female student was outshining him in some laboratory class. The image of his newspaper picture was the first to cross my mind.

The second image was of handcuffs. I felt certain that the silver half-circles I saw in that satchel were handcuffs.

The third image was of Pete and Lauren. This image was very bright and detailed, as if someone had flashed a slideshow across the screen of my brain.

My heart was pounding. I turned and faced him. My back was to the passenger seat of the car, as he held open the door."What are you waiting for?" he said. "Get in." He was still smiling, but his grin looked forced. I was frozen, I couldn't move. Part of me felt that I should run, the other part felt that such an action would be ridiculous. He grabbed my right upper arm with his left hand and gripped it tightly. The smile was gone. "I said: GET IN." His voice was a forced whisper and his face was only inches away from mine. He pushed forward with his left arm to push me down and backward, trying to force me to sit down on the seat. His face looked threatening. Now, I think of that image as a mask of evil.

Then I heard Pete yell "Charlotte!" Strong tried again to force me into sitting on the front seat, but somehow I got my arm free. I started to struggle, to try and dodge him so I could run away. Pete ran closer yelling, "Let her go! Let her go!"

Somehow I got past Strong and ran to Pete. (I may have even given Strong an elbow strike in the gut with a backfist to the face – but I can't be sure.) Pete and I ran into Schultz's. I started to shake and my teeth were chattering. Someone said, "I saw everything. I called 911."

Strong looked like he wanted to follow us for just a moment, then angrily slammed the passenger door, went to the driver's side of his car, and drove off with wheels screeching on pavement.

Police came and talked to Pete and me briefly, then told us to go home and stay there until they arrive. We're waiting for them now. My right hand is hurting, and looks bruised. I'll write more later.

Charlotte

To: Hansen, V
Date: Friday, February 27
From: Proesser, Donald V
Subject: Debriefed

Hi Veronica,

I'm writing this from my dad's email account. I think it is safe; I don't have my dad's business email in my address book. He has all of these super-encryption things on this account. But, even so... please print this off and delete it. I'll do the same.

I'm really not supposed to tell anyone, but you're in "the business" and I know you'll keep it confidential. I've got to tell someone, or I'll burst. Pete and my parents cannot deal with this now. That strikes me as VERY odd because I'm the one it happened to. But then the situation has dawned on me gradually, and they're being asked to deal with everything "all at once."

The police suspect that Strong had multiple victims. And as you would probably suspect, he had them cataloged in the "Minerva's Voice" newsletter files. However, I was unique in that I was one of the several he emailed using his own name. According to the police (and I would agree), this gave him more leverage and credibility because of my background in science and higher education. But this strategy was a risk for him, as well.

The name he used for the majority of his victims was "Phineas Oberon." I'm not sure where the "Phineas" came from, but "Oberon" is the name of the Shakespearean character in "A Midsummer Night's Dream" who tried to administer a potion to Titania while she was asleep so she would fall in love with him. He also subscribed to "LinKKet," a service that provided him with detailed information on his victims. That way, he could structure the emails to them with personal messages meant to build trust and resonate with their unconscious minds. Based on the content of some of the emails, his strategy seemed to have worked on some women. The authorities have interviewed one woman and they are working on contacting several more.

Additionally, he met with women with ties to the academic or industry side of research. He is a chemist, so he may have had an interest in products in development, possibly to profit from inside knowledge. Evidently, his "personal" type of strategy worked on several occasions. He has accounts of these meetings in his computer files. Some accounts are written notes, others are audio files.

The police feel that he is a highly skilled at what he does; they do not know if they can successfully prosecute him. The interviews with his contacts will be crucial. They will try to contact some of the victims and see if they can enlist them for prosecution in Kansas City, where many of the encounters took place. Probably several states are involved, he did travel extensively to meet some victims if he felt it was "worthwhile."

The police also told me that Strong had icons on his computer screen that connected to joke sites that featured misogyny. No surprise there.

My case may have been unique in several ways. He did have a colleague on my campus he could legitimately meet with, so he may have taken the chance on coming to campus, even though I didn't seem "enthusiastic." The police also suspect in my case, that Strong was interested in the information regarding SomaRx's new antidepressant. There were some emails from representatives from other big pharma corporations on his computer. They wonder if he planned to leak the information to someone who would be willing to pay big money for it.

Also, he most likely set up a remote access system to my computer. The police cyber-detectives found parental control software on it, and neither Pete nor I put it there. This probably allowed him access to my email accounts, so that is how he knew about me; my hair color, dress color, etc. He could know a lot about you, too. So, be careful!

They may be able to prosecute him in Indiana under an anti-stalking law. If so, I'll be the star witness. If it happens, I'll get myself ready with the help of Ray, I'm sure.

So right now, he's free. He could even leave the country. But I doubt that would happen.

Pete's been great, very protective. He hugs me at least once an hour and said last night "I can't believe I could have lost you forever." All Lauren knows is that we came to visit Grandma and Grandpa in Chicago because "Mommie was followed by a bad man, but she's safe now." My parents look at me and sigh a lot. My mother said last night: "I'm so glad that you are here." (Me, too!)

Well, as far as the punch that I wasn't sure about I must have thrown it! I have a cast on my right hand now (which means that I am "hunting and pecking" with my left to write this – you can appreciate how long that is taking me!) I broke one of the metacarpals in my right hand. The MD in the emergency department up here thinks I must have followed that elbow strike with a backfist to the face!

That's the story in a nutshell. I still have a hard time believing it myself. I feel very, very, lucky. I'm alive, I have a wonderful husband and a talented, beautiful daughter.

I'm going to stay in Chicago with my Mom and Dad for the week. Pete is going to take Lauren to his parents' house and get her to school. Then, he'll come up and get me next weekend and we'll move back to the apartment, together. We're committed to working out our problems, and he's going into counseling with me.

What an adventure life is! You've been a supportive friend through it all. Your advice definitely helped keep me sane. You may not hear from me for a week or so, but I'll be in touch when I get back to Indy.

Thanks for listening to me when no one else would.

Charlotte

About C. L. Shore

C. L. Shore is a nurse practitioner, educator, and researcher. She's the author of the mystery novel *Seeker of Truth* and several short stories. She has another full length mystery novel in progress and has plans for several more. She lives in the Indianapolis area with her family and an ornery tabby cat. Visit her website at www.clshoreonline.com.

www.ingramcontent.com/pod-product-compliance
Lightning Source LLC
Chambersburg PA
CBHW070612130626
46556CB00001B/345